C000150191

BRENDAI

METROPHILIAS

With an Introduction by

DANIEL CORRICK

THIS IS A SNUGGLY BOOK

This Snuggly Books edition is an amended version of that which was first published by Better Non Sequitur in 2010. The introduction by Daniel Corrick is original to the current edition.

ISBN: 978-1-943813-07-0

CONTENTS

INTRODUCTION

WHEN I first heard about this collection several years, ago what initially piqued my attention was, oddly enough, the format.

The vignette or prose poem has long occupied a venerable place in Western Literature. From the laconic fables of Aesop to the droll wisdom pieces of 18th century Hasidism to the tortured instances of Baudelaire's *Paris Spleen,* it has proved an apt and incisive tool, capable of cutting to the core of the chosen moment or theme where the broad ceremonial axe of the novel would have merely reduced it to pulp. Unfortunately, for one reason or another—possibly because of the spate of very bad poetry at the beginning of the Edwardian period—it has somewhat fallen out of favour amongst Anglophone writers. This is a great shame because, not only do such exercises in narrative conciseness showcase an author's abilities, they also provide a markedly different experience for the reader, one which can be most invigorating if carried off successfully. That they should have gained a reputation for 'effeteness' seems to me a matter of strange irony.

The pieces in this collection are not 'effete'. They are miniatures possessed of vibrance, cruelty and colour. Connell's style is erudite and his humour often pointed. The most obvious literary comparison would be the French novelist J.K. Huysmans: both employ certain narrative techniques such as using terms relating to the sense of taste to describe moods or systems of thought; naturalistic descriptions of the types of food characters are eating; the style of clothes people are wearing; long list-like sentences showcasing myriads of exotic items; and sensual, often lascivious, similes mixed with technical terminology (the phrase 'a painter's eye and a gourmet's tongue' comes to mind). Yet to view Connell's writing solely in the light of Huysmans would be to present a limited perspective and to do it a disservice. As with the contents themselves, one gets the impression of turning the pages of an atlas, of a stylistic Grand Tour. There are hints of Far Eastern literature, of Johnsonian Era picaresques and of High Modernism—in particular use of single word sentence statements and odd forms of punctuation such as mathematical signs reminds us of the Italian Futurists 'Abolition of Syntax'. To a field flooded with creaky teenage colloquialisms and the discharges of the 'go with what you know' school it makes for quite a change!

A cursory summary of the collection—stories of bizarre lusts and obsessions—fails to do justice to the contents. It might lead the reader to expect a series of Neo-Realist anecdotes on the corrupting effect of urban life. While there are certainly elements of this, particularly in the bleak Eastern European sections, more often than not the connection between location and pro-tagonist takes place on a more subliminal level. Each of the pieces depends upon execution as much as plot: one could say that the ranges of locations bring with them a seasoning of the representative aesthetics of that culture and period. Whether tragic intrigue in dynastic China or club-land dialogues on mediumship or lavish olfactory vignettes in ancient Sybaris, they each display a wonder-ful dexterity of style and imagination. At this point the reader might be justified in wondering whether all these changes of scene don't lead to the author's own voice be-ing submerged under the weight of History—thankfully it quickly becomes apparent that this is not the case, for on nearly every occasion the narrative is bound tightly together by a distinctive wit (to select but one instance, the phrase: 'You wish to marry a vase, I do not see the advantage in such an alliance,' has to be one of the best lines of matrimonial disapproval ever set to paper).

To draw my musings to a close and allow the reader to experience the work for themselves, I shall end by saying that *Metrophilias* is an example of the vignette done right and of the work of a fine writer. Neo-Decadent mosaic, guide book, travelogue of the jaded Eros—it presents a medley of different flavours. It gives us great pleasure to publish this new edition. We can only hope Connell will continue to produce such works in the future.

—Daniel Corrick

METROPHILIAS

ATHENS

A T 10:00 a.m. yesterday, Katia Kaltsas, aged 28, was arrested in possession of the hand of a statue dating back 2,500 years. The object had been stolen earlier this year from a private collection and was located amongst the suspect's négligées.

Over the weekend, Sapfo Fotopoulos and Giorgos Voutsinas were taken into police custody. The one for indecent exposure in the National Archaeological Museum, before the Zeus of Artemision. The other for a similar crime at the Museum of Cycladic Art.

Statuary antiquities collector Stratos Alexandrakis, 47, was stabbed three times in the chest by his wife, Sophia, 44. Reason: valid jealousy.

———

At that time the city was inhabited by men most gifted, philosophers, politicians and poets;—artists had adorned it with objects divinely beautiful. Polygnotos' paintings: of Achilles, of Odysseus; the wrestler of Timainetos.

As beautiful as all these paintings were, however, it was not to them that Tiphys devoted his enthusiasm. He was an adamant lover of sculpture, a connoisseur of marble and bronze. The Acropolis was his favourite haunt; he would perambulate the Parthenon.

One day, on the Street of the Panathenaia, he met Eubulus.

"Where are you coming from?" asked Tiphys.

"From the public latrine near the civic offices."

"Oh! I always use that in the Helaia, as it is kept significantly cleaner."

"And you, Tiphys—where are you walking from with such a contented glow to your face?"

"From the gymnasia dear boy . . . where laboriously I clutched."

"Wrestling were you?"

"No, just hugging the statues."

"Better a wife, my friend."

"Love a creature of flesh? Not I! The odour of their warm bodies is not a thing to stir my passions, while cool marble . . . —Never will I, like foolish Pygmalion, pray for my beloved statue to come to life!"

Tiphys: not long after he locked himself up in the Temple of Athena Nike and refused to come out.

Police yesterday raided homes and businesses in a giant sweep aimed at breaking up the biggest ring of statuary prostitution in the city. 23 suspects were arrested and another 14 are being sought. 19 ancient statues were recovered.

4

BARCELONA

"WHAT could have happened to him?"
"God only knows."
"Ah, the poor girl."

Señora Martinez looked sadly at her daughter, Pilar, who sat rigid in the high-backed chair of the anti-room, her white wedding gown spilling around her and tears from her eyes; a young lady beautiful enough that even the priest could not control his leer and she brought out impulses amorous in men every time they saw her, whether they were ancient types of seventy or more years or young of sixteen.

Someone, some villain, maniac or coward, had done this to her on the day of ceremony when she was supposed to be blended with him.

But let us go back, nine short weeks:

Alfredo Granados was an intelligent young man with a warm smile and a kind-hearted manner. Though his face was somewhat too linear, his nose too large for him to be called handsome, he was still the sort of man who women easily fall in love with—for he had a romantic and loyal nature and most women will always take a loyal man over a handsome, one romantic over one whose thoughts are over-crowded with lust.

Alfredo wore a green short-sleeved shirt and a pair of brown slacks. He sat with his friend, Diego de Falla, in the latter's fourth-floor apartment on the Carrer Ample, just a holler away from the Rambla.

"So, in two months you will be a married man!"

Alfredo smiled.

"Yes," he said, "you will have to find someone else to keep you company on Saturday nights."

"There is something tragic about marriage. It is like watching a man being buried alive."

"Come now, we still have two months worth of drinking to do. That's quite a few bottles of wine."

"Hey, I am not going to see my best friend buried alive with mundane wine in his stomach."

"Eh?"

"Tonight we are going to drink something different."

"Anything you pour me I will drink."

Diego rose from his seat, went to the kitchen and presently returned with a tray on which sat two Duralex glasses, a jug of heavily iced water, a little bowl of sugar cubes, two perforated spoons and a bottle of absinthe.

Alfredo frowned.

"Damn, I thought you meant to give me Champagne."

"Carbonated beverages are for women," Diego said as he poured a little of the light green liquid into each glass. He then placed the spoon on the glass and a cube of sugar on the spoon. With infinite care he let the water trickle over the sugar. The liquid began to cloud, to louche.

"To your future," he said, as he clicked glasses with Alfredo.

The latter, with the same hesitation as a man dipping his foot into a cold lake before taking a plunge, took the smallest of sips.

"It tastes like rubber," he said, making a face.

Diego laughed.

"No, your taste-buds just aren't acclimatised. You are like a fish seller's wife who has been given roses and complains of the smell."

Alfredo again put the glass to his lips. The liquid, faintly anise flavoured, ran over his tongue, caused a slight tingling before encountering his throat, which it bit the back of. Presently he felt a tickling in his lips then fingertips then toes. He could feel something in his belly, like a creature moving around, spreading its warm tendrils through him.

"It has a pleasant effect, but it is not very intoxicating," he said, looking at Diego keenly.

"It shouldn't be."

Alfredo, feeling vaguely mystical, smiled, felt the cool glass in the palm of his hand, his intoxication gradual as are certain obsessions, but his obsession was sudden.

The first week was one of complete indulgence. Going from bar to bar, sharp corners losing their edges against the dahlias that spilled from his eyes and then he would go home and cuddle up in bed for a few hours beneath sky-blue sheets before, surprisingly clear-headed and with a faint smile on his lips, he rose and made his way to work.

He still saw Pilar, though admittedly less and her friends told her not to worry, because men are always like that in the weeks before matrimony, and when he did see her there were so many arrangements to be done that they barely had time to exchange lips.

But no matter, for now there was nothing, no vows, no veil, no hope, that separated him from his dreams.

There were clouds.

And this new discovery opened before him new lands, vast forests and plains that existed inside his own mind—whole solar systems in which ideas collided and crackled like fireworks. All those liquor stores he had previously passed without so much as turning his head, those shops with dusty shelves and shop-men who smelled like rotting carrots, now seemed to him like the most interesting places in the world, and he would spend hours together gazing in the windows at the colourful and complex displays of bottles in all shapes and sizes, the labels of which showed everything from naked maidens lounging on green grass to devils rising up from scorching flames—hundreds of modern disciples of Dr. Ordinaire's original creation. Some bottles were dark green, the colour of jade, others playful blue, like the eyes of German virgins, others showed decorations of flowers, others wild animals—tigers, elephants or monkeys. There were those, vaguely oriental, that made him think of foreign lands perfumed by sandalwood and dressed in turbans, while others, displaying nude women with small breasts and large hips, made him feel as if he were in the presence of nymphs.

And, naturally, the more he saw the more he wanted.

He sucked at the breast of this thing, withdrawing from it white nectar as delicious as the juice of a ripe moon.

His thoughts became as mellow as butterflies floating over the flames of his blood.

He picked up the glass and drank snails, giving himself the enjoyment of every sip.

He panted like a dog and for another.

This was the drink that Ulysses used to intoxicate Polyphemus and, when he added water, the liquid would begin to dance; black, Gothic style absinthe, highly alcoholic, with its faint taste of roses, and the showy bottles glittering with bright-coloured liquid which tended, like low-end prostitutes, to lack the skill necessary to make him feel the most sublime inertia—an ability reserved to the simple clear liquids of high proof, replete with thujone; cold water added, its eyes clouded over with a passionate mist and they combined and he lost himself in the agitated calm of its body pleasant and bitter-sweet, milky, almost grey, with only the slightest hint of green.

So, while tears were falling from the eyes of his fiancée, Alfredo was letting the day pass without a care, with hardly a thought of the mortal in wedding vestments he had left behind as he held between the arms of his lips a thing which answered wishes he had never even known he had had. A woman cried in a church. A man looked at his drink as it louched, seeing sunsets in his glass, green forests, waves crashing on sea-anemone-inhabited shores.

And when he laughed, his laughter was sharp and without regret and the days passed, naturally, effortlessly, and long nights in which meditation vied with joy and usually he looked like anyone else, his nose held high, his gaze clear and then he steps through his door, undoes his tie, takes off his shoes, puts on a pair of straw sandals and proceeds to go about the first-drink-of-the-evening ritual.

He will continue to drink, to slide his tongue over its milky emerald thighs; then, eventually, will no longer bother with sugar, will have had enough of diluting it with water, and will drink it neat, frenzied. And when he collapses, after another orgasm of absinthe, vertebrae shaking, marrow enflamed, in a puddle of piss in some slim unlit alley, happiness will settle over him like a cloud of lace as on all sides the city roars with the sounds of its eternal fiesta, thoughts flying sharp and straight as arrows to the stars.

BENARES

TEMPLES, so many, rising out of the mass of houses, hovels, palaces, the air thick with the smoke of incense and burning corpses; the air filled with chanted prayers, activity of life. Boats and satchels of human ash float upon Mother Ganges.

Somadatta bathed himself in the Manikarnika Ghat, that pit which Vishnu had dug with his chakra and filled with the sweat of his meditation. Ascetics lined the banks of the river; some naked, hairless, skeletal, adorned with nothing but strings of beads; others covered with great manes, crouching like famished dogs, dressed in nothing but ashes. There were those who sat on beds of spikes, and those whose loins were encased in chastity belts of copper. One man held his right arm, wasted, shrunken, constantly towards the sky, having vowed not to lower it for twelve years. Another stood with a pot of fire on his head.

Somadatta had let his nails and hair grow out. For him it was taboo to eat ginger or sugar-cane; it was taboo for him to oil his body or garnish it with even the simplest ornament. And he was not an eater of living things; for him all living things were precious.

He now turned from the river and walked, with measured steps. The women he passed, their ankles jingling with bangles, their toes glittering with silver rings, he did not let his glance stray to. He avoided the streets where he knew existed the enclosures of harlots;—he walked, making sure his glance was even and straight before him, not straying towards either earth or sky. He passed by the hundred-foot-high statue of Shiva Mahesvara, which was made of shining brass. He passed by vendors of perfume and vendors of spice, by leprous beggars and princes whose turbans were decorated with richly-hued peacock feathers. From shaded alleys came the sound of grammarians reciting Panini; from rooftops the cackle of bickering wives.

Soon he came to the patch of ground surrounding a certain sacred temple. Peepul and sirísaka trees. A cow resting. Quiet.

Somadatta sat upon the earth and crossed one leg over the next. Unlike the general practitioner of meditation, he did not in-draw his senses, but rather, gradually, let his consciousness melt into a single one. That of touch. His skin.

An ant crawled over his foot, its antennae quivering. Somadatta's tongue crept out of his mouth and moistened his lips. A fly alighted on the tip of his nose. Sentient beings. Ants. Flies. Attracted to his oils, his sweat. They were now coming to him, touching his skin. A file along the earth. The aerial causeway from the cow to him. Others might crush them, or flick them away, but he would not. Yes, at one time every single one of those ants had been a woman, as beautiful as any in all of Bharata. At one time, each of those flies had been a goddess, endowed with breasts like dual moons, and sweetly scented for extreme bliss. Could he deny their advances, these creatures who, in their former lives had been sought after by the greatest kings, by powerful gods? The delicate touch of their thousands of feet, six-jointed legs, the glancing of their tibial spurs, was to him exquisite. Pleasure givers. Pulvilli. Vomiting saliva. Tickling labella. They began to cover his body, those numerous beings—and he, he gasped in ecstasy,—the ecstasy of the cosmic orgy.

BERLIN

HER name was Trude. The zone she lived in has been inhabited since the Stone Age. Her eyes were two sharp dabs of ocean cobalt. The city, a flood of bricks and steel, spills out over an area of 890 sq km. Her hair was stolen from the sun. Scene bars dreary decadence in exotic greys. Hillocks of white flesh packaged in off-fashion rayons and hose.

She liked that sense of well-seasoned maturity. Strength smooth masculinity dome molten brains. That cleanliness of the head. Virile moon feel sweat heart monolith gush yes she was a woman of particular *needs*.

"I have certain requirements," she said.

It was smooth surfaces she loved, shining craniums, scalps devoid of hair, streaked with networks of veins, bold boulders yolk ancient crop earth-rite pyramidion greasy roars sparkle crack.

There was a little man named Felix whose head was like a billiard ball. His eyes were soft and he looked very gentle. At night he would beat her. She adored him. He grew bored and left her. When she looked in the mirror, it seemed to her that her tears were pink.

It was a week later that she met Cort. Two metres of tough tissue. Head of a rocket. He carried her in his arms and sprinkled her with kisses. What a gentleman! A human obelisk. When he fell on one knee and proposed to her she kissed the top of his head. In the Kreuzberg district he was stabbed three times and robbed applaud granata narcotic scrawl bright lights of dark corners.

Willow trees like big shaggy heads of hair. Luminous energy licked water. She walked in Görlitzer Park. The eastern end, near the little pond. The water glistened, but so did his cranium. He got up when he saw her. Undisguised.

"My name is Wilhelm."

"And I am Trude."

"Why do you walk alone?"

"Because I am alone."

"No, you are with me."

"Yes, we can walk together."

"You are not looking into my eyes."

"No."

"Do you prefer a man with hair?"

"Never."

Concrete.

The well-oiled head of a bald man would send her into an almost epileptic fit.

CARTHAGE

THE city sits beneath the sword-like rays of the pulsing sun; it sits against an ocean blue to profundity, shores gently lashed by the trillion fins of that vast creature, air swept by seagulls' wings. Its internal harbour is crowded with huge galleys. Its walls are twenty-three miles in circuit. Narrow, winding streets, many-storied dwellings, the murmur of commerce, the smell of incense and bake house blend together, as the bleating of sacrificial animals does with the thriving laughter of whores.

The merchant princes of this city are cruel and each has an abundance of chained slaves. The people are prosperous and, fed on the paste of nuts and half-cooked meat, like their love piquant. So when that sun-drenched metropolis becomes a lunar city and darkness blows itself through the streets, the citizens, penetrating into their dwellings, begin by candle and torch light their masquerades.

Some wear masks made of ostrich eggs, others of terra cotta, the richest citizens masks of silver, ivory and gold. Red, green, black—each picks a colour suited to temperament, a shade of fantasy. Some are fringed with dried grasses, others with feathers—many highlighted with bright glossy beads. One has a long, thin beard, blue in colour, which hangs to the floor, wags like a lizard's tail; another enormous eyebrows, like the wings of a crow.

Lips twisted in hideous grins.

Under the mask a timid woman becomes a demoness, a haughty merchant a weeping child. Some, with the faces of animals, give their bestiality free reign. Others assume the aspect of gods and let out furious screams as they pursue the course of their bizarre romances. The force of fertility foams like the mouth of a hard-driven horse, goaded on by the power of transformation, the power of persona.

A male torso; the mask of a crocodile. The creature wobbles around the room, its prey a heavy-bosomed female whose face is that of a fish. The former pushes his tapered snout forward; the latter agitates her fins, her arms, the wrists of which are bangled with gold. The faintest murmur issues from the puckered hole of her lips—she is begging to be eaten alive. Needless to say, the predator complies.

We lift off the roof of a nearby mansion, see within a party of evil spirits. One has the horns of an antelope, a second those of a bull. A huge-chested, narrow-hipped man flaunts a horse-hair headdress. Truncated mouths above which jut large, upturned noses. Some have javelin teeth, some tusks. A fat woman has the head of a mule, pink flamingo feathers spewing from her ears. These beings dance like cyclones, embrace like frenzied serpents. Enwrapped in the venom of lust, bathed in a hesitating yellow light, these disguised, like beings erupted from the dens of the earth, revel in unbridled indulgence of passions.

Now down the way, towards the docks, there is a humbler dwelling, that of a common oarsman. He too, however, enjoys his night-time frolic. For when drooling darkness tongues his outer walls, and the narrow alleys of his neighbourhood are abandoned by all but sharp-toothed rats, he sits within, his only bodily clothing the avid embrace of his mistress. But what is this? The disk of baked clay that covers her face represents that of a beautiful woman. The oarsman's own features are hidden behind a piece of painted wood, a piece of wood painted with the face of a handsome, smiling youth. They live out their fantasy of beauty—him whose nose was lopped off for being surly to a high-ranking officer; her whose face is a scar-scribbled loaf.

In Carthage they cultivate the mystery of love.

DUBLIN

IN the city of Dublin there is a group of erotic-pyromaniacs. They are excited by fire. They gather in apartments in high buildings and, after drinking scaltheen, that rich mixture of whisky and rancid butter, set alight birds and small animals doused in the same.

They are the New Hellfire Club.

Sometimes they build a bonfire in a yard and take turns leaping through the flames.

Pleasures from the innocent to the extreme.

Some are students from Trinity College. Others are middle-aged doctors, minor government officials, or again barmaids. They all have strong passions and imaginative dispositions.

In the deep of night they sneak off in groups of three, four; up to half a dozen. To begin the fun they strike matches. They giggle and strike matches. Like the ancient Canaanites, they too find more than just heat in those flames.

Fire is the mediator between earth and heaven. Worshippers of Vulcan, worshippers of Ixcoçauhqui, of Agni.

A restaurant went to blazes in Temple Bar; a fully occupied house near St. Stephen's Green.

On Northbrook Road. An old bacon factory. Some sticks and paper piled together before the door. One young man arrives with a can of petrol. The two women who are there rub up against him, kiss him, whisper erotic endearments. Now together they wet the place with fuel.

A grave looking gentleman with a huge moustache, the oldest of the party, lights a cigar, and puffs. The smoking stick goes from mouth to mouth—sucked on, stained with lip-stick. Then against the papers it smoulders, watched with excitement. Smoke. A little flame. And it begins to burst forth.

As the flames rise up, enveloping the building, crackling, sending forth bursts of sparks, the little group jumps and laughs, the men like fauns, the women auloniads, each and every one thoroughly titillated by the spectacle, revelling in this antique luxury.

The screech of the siren. The fire-brigade arrives: with their hoses and curses. But by then the erotic-pyromaniacs are already back in their drab brick dwellings—drinking a grog, toddling off to bed. After a night of eccentric enjoyment.

EDINBURGH

THE place—a dreary-coloured four-storey building—was on Meadowband Terrace, opposite the
Meadowband Stadium.

Inspector Young worked his huge body up the stairs,
panting after the first flight, puffing after the second—
wheezing, wiping his forehead with a handkerchief by
the time he had reached the top.

An officer stood in front of the door. The inspector waved him aside and entered. He found himself in
the front room of a compact, loft apartment. A second
officer sat at a table and was filling out a report. The
adjoining room was open and the inspector could make
out a large stripe of white skin dangling from one of the
rafters.

The officer looked up. Young threw himself into a
chair and exhaled.

"Damned stairs," he said. Then, motioning towards
the body: "Who is he?"

"A nobody. A civil servant. A suicide."

"No question about it, eh?"

The officer shrugged his shoulders. "Ah don't think so. He left an, um, note."

"Let's see it."

The officer pointed to a few sheets of paper on the table.

The inspector picked the letter up and read the following:

> *To whom it may or may not concern—to whomso-ever it is that must deal with the mess I've made,*
>
> *You are reading my last letter. I have killed myself, as many before me have done, because of disappointment in love. How blasé it sounds! But, God knows, my passion is anything but blasé.*
>
> *If it had only been one of those rare letters that do not eternally invade our diction—an X or a Z;—if it had been one of those, I might not now have to be writing this letter of farewell. But fate would not be fate if——*
>
> *But let me carry on.*
>
> *My parents were both neuropathic. I myself have always been a nervous type. My stutter. The tic in my left eye. Yet I am intelligent and have always been sensitive and used to cry like the rain. On the shoulder of my nanny. Her name was Wendy—sometimes she wore a blouse with a W appliquéd onto the left breast, over her heart. Needless to say I was in love with her. After all, don't all little boys fall in love with their nannies?*
>
> *I don't know where she went, but I do know*

that I used to take the keenest pleasure in running my fingers over that letter.

Let's move on.

My problem became openly manifest around the age of thirteen. I dreamt of it—not of her—but that thing stitched to her blouse.

In High School and at University I dated women and visited prostitutes—those creatures that stand under black umbrellas on Salamander Street—but found myself to be wholly ineffective, absolutely impotent. This was all the more troubling as my mind was constantly invaded by licentious thoughts and my disposition was decidedly romantic.

When I contemplated it, when I saw it in large, bold type, I would be overcome by an intensely lustful feeling. I won't bother cataloguing my fantasies. Let it simply be said that they were of the most ebullient nature. It was the thing I wanted, with its lovely curves—like two neighbouring valleys of concupiscence. That semivowel of horns became for me not merely a representation of love, but the object itself.

I tried to beat the lubricious thoughts from my mind, but they continuously returned, seeming to always gain in force, and it was apparent that my very soul and sanity were in danger.

In an attempt to control my perversity, I began seeing a young woman by the name of Wanda. She was twenty-four, with red hair, good teeth and green eyes, and kept herself pretty well. To aid me in my endeavour, I bought her a blouse and had a seamstress stitch the letter W over the left breast. I could tell that Wanda was not thrilled when she saw the thing. She apparently thought it was in bad taste—but wore it anyway to please me. This attracted me greatly and I made advances to which she responded eagerly. Unfortunately she insisted on taking off the blouse. I begged her to leave it on. At first she laughed at me but, when I persisted, she grew angry and then cold. She told me I could take my stutter elsewhere, and I did. After all, it was not a woman I wanted, but a letter made of flesh which I could throw my arms around, sink my hungry teeth into.

How often I have wandered through the streets, walked from my flat to the Castle and back, trying to tire myself out, distract myself. I have spent hours at St. Mary's, my knees bent in prayer, only to leave, look up at the spires of that great church and be once more reminded of my beloved letter.

How many pints I have drunken, how many glasses of grog! But my bizarre fascination always floats on the surface of my thoughts and cannot be drowned.

My perverse fancy for that divine letter has led me to commit all sorts of absurdities. Sometimes, on a clear night, I go to Calton Hill and gaze up at the five stars of Cassiopeia—shivering with lust! At other times I stalk the Royal Mile, in the wild hope of seeing some mortal woman whose limbs are properly twisted to my demands.

Hopeless.

Oh, how I would like to bury myself in its un-dulations! Every time I write it—WWWWW—I feel a spasm of longing! A longing which, alas, can never be satisfied. Those two overturned mounds, so eloquently resembling the dangling breasts of a woman—or then again, like legs flung in the air. That esurient spike which rises up in your middle. Oh, pornographic letter! W! The culmination of all that is beautiful in this world. If I could only impregnate you . . .

It is impossible to describe how unhappy I am. This moral affliction controls my entire life—fills me with disgust for it. I am always restless. I trem-ble and cannot sleep. I have not an ounce of self-esteem left, and see no choice before me but the one I am about to take.

Sincerely,
Donald Abercromby

The inspector set down the sheets of paper with a grunt. He turned. Two men in white jackets had entered and were now taking the body down. Inspector Young heaved himself out of his seat and waddled into the next room—the bedroom. The men lay the body down on the sea grass carpeting. It was thin, delicately made. The head was small and symmetrical. The torso: a large, bleeding *W* had been carved into the left breast with a razor.

FLORENCE

ANTA MARIA NOVELLA. The day of San Bruno.
Domenico Ghirlandaio's *Scenes from the Life of the Virgin.* Filippino Lippi (that son of Carmelite monk + pretty
novice): the bright and beautiful colour of his frescoes,
depicting: St. Phillip: driving the dragon from the Temple of Hieropolis; St. John the Evangelist: resuscitating
Druisana—(these made all the more brilliant by the tenebristic interior of the church).

. . . Now the Gondi Chapel, where a young woman
(named Geronima) had been contemplating Brunelleschi's crucifix. Her skin was very white, her face delicately modelled, her hair dyed golden and plucked about
the forehead, as were the brows of her eyes. A fine silk
veil covered her shoulders. Her dress, which was laced up
the front, was light-red in colour and had loose purple
sleeves embroidered with a floral motif. Her feet were in
shoes of velvet. Her right hand held a rosary of twelve
carved apricot kernels alternating with twelve gold and
enamel beads and adorned with a small silver cross set
with pearls.

She turned, stepped, found herself before that other, that which had been painted by the young Giotto, and now hung from the ceiling above her, and she gazed up, furthering her rapture; at: the pale green body of Christ, pinned to that magnificent shape, gold-edged, potent and complex.

"Ah, she is so religious," all who saw her would say, little suspecting that the thoughts filling her mind were the very opposite of pure.

Her first awakenings of womanhood were accompanied by religious devotions, by prayers to the rightful cross—an object which indeed represented for her all that was masculine.

Because, when she looked on it, that divinely phallic object, she had no need to gaze on man.

Her father kept her from the public eye, but did not keep her from the churches—of which she went from one to the next, viewed the numerous roods, some crusted in jewels,—in rubies, emeralds and cornelian,—some made of wood, some cut out of panels and painted. In the Baptistery there was that on the altar of San Giovanni, in shining silver, the work of Bernardo Cennini. In Santa Croce there were the crucifixes of Cimabue and Donatello. Indeed these were the things she pictured: entering, piercing her, filling her with rapture. . . .

(She longed for it, that upright thing, in ways most intimate.)

She prostrated before the cross, adored it as though the Saviour were there in flesh, leaking blood and hanging upon it, and she would gladly have fastened herself to that item.

"I want to escape from the miseries of the world and join a nunnery," she told her father.

But she being his only child, he would not hear of it.

She was married to Ferrante de' Nerli, a handsome, long-shanked man somewhat above his thirtieth year.

Their wedding night:

Bellies full from banqueting; him merry from drinking. Brocaded hangings. A sumptuous bed, above which it hung. Enamelled. Gold. Blue. Green. That dying figure, wearing the golden crown of the King of Heaven, was surrounded by the three virtues—Faith, Charity, and Hope. A Eucharistic chalice, placed below his feet, caught his blood. Red.

"No . . . do not," she said.

"I was only going to put out the candle."

"No."

"I was thinking of you . . ."

"No."

Unfastening feeling of crushed silk girdle.

". . . my Lord the opener . . ."

. . . mother of all saints meets father of thousands crutched hymen opener cruciate fertilisation symbolic of generation . . . gazed at the cross which hung above their bed. . . . And so it was. . . .

Later, he died from wounds received in a duel. Geronima took the news with little emotion, showed dry eyes. As she was still young, and without child, it was expected that she would seek for another husband, but she did not.

Her eccentricity: During the day her eyes would continually stray to it, continually she would cast its way amorous sheep-eyed glances. At night she would take it down, flirt with it, pay homage, touch her lips to it. Sometimes she would dress it up, in little costumes, indeed strongly resembling in miniature form those her husband had worn. Geronima held the cross to her, pressed to her bosom, undressed what she had dressed, now felt it cold against her skin. She hugged it. . . . That cross she would coax with adoration and fondle . . . letting it take her to paradise.

GWANGJU

MRS. YIM held the phial of spice, that dark pinkish powder in her fingers. Yes, it was running low.

"Like an hourglass," she thought, with a melancholy smile, noting the way the sun hit the green leaves outside, shining through, and illuminating them.

Her husband had been older than herself; a grim and laconic man. (A crocodile, a snake, a bear.) Yes—he had certainly been of bulk—magnitude. And it was he who had torn those ligaments—and given her firsthand knowledge of intimate implosion. . . . An idol to worship. . . . A religion all her own.

The terror she had felt on his passing was genuine. . . . A naked and vulnerable being, suspended in the cold of space. . . . He was no longer there to scold her; to form a breathing mass beneath her blanket.

The fruit out of grasp.

The beans stolen.

The tree?

Chopped.

And that had been no easy task.

It had taken doing. And even a bribe. To ascertain that lump of dough, that cake, or gobbet. —And, naturally, she had felt remorseful—sending that spirit into the hereafter without its, possibly, most valuable asset. But everyone is entitled to be selfish at times and she was simply a woman unwilling to part with a certain earthly treasure.

The silver casket she had set on her dresser, the inside lined with velvet, the object of her desire lodged within. When certain friends of her sex visited, she would take it out, let them fondle the dried specimen, and then retrieve it with a jealous laugh.

Its mere presence gave her pleasure, its touch nigh on bliss, ravishment—a hedonic quivering which she found delectable . . . let grace her flesh with it in the evening— glance it here; press, kiss and dimple there . . . under the dim light of her bedside lamp. . . . Memory conjoined to fantasy.

Yes, others might choose what they would: even rude and filthy roots: turnips, daikons or yams. . . . But, to her, love was linked solely to him, and his severing.

Yet time brought with it mildews, which disturbed, undermined the architecture. . . . The stalk splintered— the sacred relic, it too a transient thing—could no longer be used with aggressive motion, or lent delectable impetus. . . . But of those shards came the cure, the medicine, so efficacious, which on rare occasion she offered sample to others, but largely kept to herself, as she was a more or less possessive wife, or even widow.

That object of love was ground in a mortar of stone, and the powder sent forth an aroma, so very heady, so

31

very much that of man. It caused her genuine titillation, to once again experience the perfume of the grim Flower Knight—to unleash those locked away essences—those vibratory impulses dilating her nostrils, as her hand manipulated the pestle.

The powder was more than just precious—it was her absolute link, to him, the culmination, physical, emotional, that instance of experience, intense and unrestrained. . . . She crimsoned with wonder. . . . Bathed in moisture. . . . Mixed those grains with warm water, a spoonful of sugar. . . . Ambrosia of a solitary woman.

At first she took those doses nightly—living in a near constant swoon of dreamy excitement. Later she held herself back, knowing full well her supply was limited . . . She restrained herself, moved hastily from place to place, a whirl of nervous spontaneity, activity—now rushing off to go shopping at Geumnamno; now taking advantage of the cultural walk at Jungoe Park.

But one could not be forever out and about.

And when the release came, the laconic one was there, to listen, and enjoy the dark sighs of breath.

Tender, almost painful. . . . Awakening the other side of the night. . . . That operation. . . . The boiling in her veins.

"Yes," she thought, looking at the dwindling phial by the light of the window, "I must certainly try and make this last another spring, last until the royal azaleas bloom on Mt. Mudeung once again."

Because, she knew full well, that she could not live without him.

HAVANA

THE pigeon he had had sent up earlier. It stood in its cage, cooed, and pecked at the pile of seed set on the newspaper before it. Out of the three hundred and four species, Señor Negrín certainly had picked out the most drab, the *Columba livia*, the rock dove, better known as the common street pigeon.

Vilma lay back on the overly soft mattress, a coil of smoke pluming from the nearby ashtray, where the stalk rested / the bitter dew / or venom of snake.

Yes, she had experienced much in her half-life. . . . The initiations. . . . The predilections. . . . Was it for coin of the realm? . . . Altruism? . . . (Always vulgar, always horror, thirst and hunger.)

"Come in," she called at the knock, her expression changing, again, without grudge, ready for that fifth and final act, the disruption.

Señor Negrín entered, impressive, composed, his presence filling up the room. He twisted the culebra, flat and braided, between his index finger and thumb, advanced it to his lips, and puffed. Yes, he was adept at that, holding it firm and straight, his mouth dry.

"Good, it arrived," he said, nodding toward the birdcage.

With face slightly flushed he stepped to the bed, and set his half-finished cigar next to the smouldering cigarette. The perfume, a veritable incense, collided with that odour, of whose head was smeared with the red of her lips. He removed his blazer; she tucked in her legs; and he set it down where they had been.

"Do you think you'll need to?" she asked.

"Quiet."

The man, undoing his tie, advanced to the cage. The bird within pecked at the seed, cooed, and turned its head, throat glossy, shimmering purple and turquoise. What he, Negrín, had done in his youth (a somewhat too delicate specimen, of narrow chest, underdeveloped cranium, chubby cheeks)—the cat in his path kicked; baseball, bat in hand; watching dogs fight (as blister burst); and them, the others, in the square, the chase, the laugh, the touch. Pseudo-hemothymia; the strip of silk drops; the cage door opens.

The wings beat against that copper epidermis, with snow of grey down; vehement, uttered in weeping lamentation; and the thing was grasped; drawn out; sampled; diameter calculated . . . immersed in it.

Tendons strained, knuckles white—his burden drops to the ground; the square is littered. . . . . A quick, convulsive effort to breathe.

And thus it was that Señor Negrín was able to reduce the monument to shambles.

She trembled.

A double corona.

ISTANBUL

MINARETS rise from a seemingly endless heap, slashed in two by the Bosporus, stabbed in the side by the Golden Horn, pushed against by the Marmora sea.

Fish being grilled on rocking boats. Tides of traffic ebbing and flowing. Tea served in teardrop-shaped cups and roasted chickens displaying their shiny skins in windows while men methodically wash their feet before prayer.

- Loom woven
- Felted textile
- Vigorous in motif and pattern

The Grand Bazaar: Anything on earth can be bought here, from sandals with sequins to plastic toys, from lilac-coloured candies, to hundred-year-old bird guns.

"You ask too much," Tarik Girik said.

"But you will never find another like this!"

"This could be true, but five thousand liras is still rather dear."

"It is half what it is worth."

"I might give you three thousand."

"And I might not accept this, as I could not go down more than five hundred."

"Very well, thirty-five hundred it is."

"You are a regular customer, a connoisseur, so I will let you rob me. Four thousand, and you may walk out of here a happy man."

The deal done, a spare-fleshed assistant wrapped the item up (a carpet in the shape of a flower, a dazzling splendour of colourful fibres, a red stolen from sunsets, a blue which seemed as if extracted from the sky).

Tarik returned to his home (a palace of sorts) a happy man indeed.

His servant laid it out in the tea room, and in that place, on that thing, he later met a young woman whose flesh was as pliant as dough.

- He had carpets for every adventure, for every mood
- Rich of tone
- Warm of colour

On the full moon of every month he would have a rendezvous in the Meadow Room. The chamber was empty except for a very strange carpet, the green-dyed silk tufts of which were so long as to make it resemble a field full of grass. Indeed, laying there with her, it seemed as if he could smell the spring and he felt rejuvenated, felt like a young colt.

But, just as men are not always young, the moon is not always full and there were times when he had recourse to a piece woven from the feathers of flamingos and times when he threw himself onto a carpet with a phyto-morphous pattern.

He had a carpet which had been woven from strands of human hair, and another from spider silk. There was a small carpet in his bedroom composed of the sinews of a bull and another in his reading room, the shape of a pomegranate blossom, made from pineapple fibre.

- Coconut fibre
- Mohair
- Raffia, woven from the palm

One night the shadow of the earth laid itself against the white skin of the moon.

Tarik Girik could not be found here or there. In a dirty storeroom he was, rolled up in a carpet woven from the coarsest catgut—so coarse indeed that when pampered skin touched the stuff, it would burst open and begin to bleed.

JERUSALEM

THE silver trumpets of the priests wake me, but I do not pray. I wet my swollen throat with water and, in my nakedness, eat of bread. In the Upper City they might breakfast on, for all I know, the food of angels, but down here, by the Dung Gate, we stuff our mouths in the morning with unleavened loaves. After wiping the crumbs from my beard, I put on my cloth and sandals, take up my rule, sling my toolbox over my shoulder;—now I, Raguel, leave my door. The Lord made me large, sturdy, a veritable giant among men. I am Raguel.

He stretched his limbs, then rubbed his eyes, then rubbed his left hand over his powerful chest.

I look up at the girdle of hills which surround the Holy City and see the dawn breaking, her soft light slipping over the walls. A faint hint of red. I go—pass by my neighbours who are just starting to do their work in ringing brass. Through the narrow streets I go, pass by the vendors, setting up their wares—crockery, baskets, cloths, rugs: all sorts of things to covet,—then through the district of the perfume factories—can smell their morning work; and I open my eyes wide.

I am Raguel and I search for my day's labour. In this city even a beggar can live well. But I am Raguel, son of Zippor, and I search for labour. For a slothful man is compared to a filthy stone.

With broad steps he strode through the narrow streets, waving the rule above his head—bait for those in need of a carpenter.

The streets of this city, this greatest of cities, are crowded— with men and women of all ranks, of all walks of life—yet of the latter, none to attract my attention. I see the rich colours of one lady's vestments. She wears silk worth its weight in gold. Another is dressed in rags. Some are ugly, some handsome. Some smell like camels, others like flowers; but no matter—use oil of violet or burn bran for fragrance, it is the same to me. I am Raguel and do not see the delightful blemish, that for which I yearn. —I am Raguel and search for my daily labour. I am Raguel and I pass by the dealers in uncooked cereals, hear the people thick around me, porters, slaves, barbers, confectioners, reed-mat makers, mail-clad warriors and squabbling accountants.

A man approached him. "You there, of the rule— you work well do you?"

"I work well and cheaply."

"Your skills?"

"I am Raguel, maker and repairer of beds, chairs, stools, tables, cabinets and chests. I can repair chariots. I can make games and toys, inlay things with pretty decorations and paint them as well."

"How much for your day?"

"A denarius plain and simple."

"Then you will do. Come now, follow me."

He is well dressed, in a turban and a long white robe set with fringes. He is of effeminate aspect, but if a eunuch I know not. I am Raguel and I follow him—up, past the theatre, into the area of palaces and towards the towers. Then there is a gate which together we go through. We pass through richly engraved doors, into a vestibule and then a large room cool and clean and well furnished where he leaves me and goes into an adjoining chamber.

I look around. The walls are covered with costly hangings. My sandals keep me poised atop a valuable carpet. House of the rich—where I will earn money to fatten my bones. I am Raguel and I will labour.

And now I hear his voice, his haughty voice turned humble. He is apparently talking to his mistress. I can hear her speak, in sounds sweet but tainted. She obviously comes from foreign parts. Whether a visitor or the lady of the establishment I know not, nor care. For my hunger is stirred by fresh bread and roasted meat; my heart by she who will not kick. Until her of my dreams comes to give me suck, I will drink the milk of goat—better by far than milk of four-appendaged prostitute, veritable poison of asp.

Wrapped in his white robe, he is here. And he summons me and I pass into the next room, and from that room there is an uncovered passageway leading to another room. And I have no time to so much as glance into that other room, for the room I am now in has a bed and I am instructed to fix it.

"Be quick, industrious and be paid and gone. Certain important tasks have been committed to my person. I will, soon enough, return and inspect your work and, if it has been done to satisfaction, put in your hand a denarius so you may leave."

It is made of carob wood and handsome Lebanese cedar and is inlaid with African ebony. And, unlike so many, its wool is not crawling with vermin. The bed is a fine piece of handiwork, but the tenons have come undone. I am Raguel the carpenter and I begin my job, contemplating on the intimacy of the place where it I do. She is in the next chamber; I know she is. For I hearken and hear her ply amongst her silks.

He worked. His copper tools pecked at, scraped against the wood. Slaves came and went. One carried a plate of sweets and figs and raisins to the room beyond; another a flagon of water. He worked, repairing the joints, strengthening them and making them good.

And now the place is still. The presence in the next chamber though I feel. And I desire to see the woman for whom I work. The apartments are yoked in silence. I am Raguel the carpenter and I crawl across the floor, then along a short passageway. And I peek, but can only see cushions piled on rugs.

And now behold, I notice! What vineyard is this!

Behold, I see her there, and she is like an egg wrapped in precious cloth, a most perfect specimen, a conduit into the garden of pleasure. Her form is blemished to perfection. She sits, a condiment set on costly cushions. The tempest is in me. The tidings of my eyes go to my brain, the tidings of my brain to my heart. And I veins are now, of a sudden, as if on fire. And I must taste the fastness of her valley.

And I cast aside my chisel. And I enter. And her eyes are as wide as sesame cakes. And she says that she will call for her slaves, but she does not call—she who makes all other women appear as spittle, whose mouth is more tempting than wine and oil.

41

I take her up in my arms. She cries out weakly, like an ewe lamb. I put one hand over her mouth, hold her tightly with the other. And I tell her not to worry, for I am Raguel, a large man, a lover of amputees and limbless women. And I lick her as the ox licks the grass of the field.

KIEV

S OILED paper, broken crockery, bits of old bread, wads of packing tape.

Stick in hand, Malevich rummaged through the trash. He was a pensioner receiving from the government five hundred and forty-four hyrvnias a month. Through rag picking, scavenging, he earned another one hundred fifty or two hundred hyrvnias.

He had mittens on his hands; was shabbily dressed. Steam issued from his lips, from beneath his grey moustache. In a shadowed alley off Andreevsky Slope, he rummaged through the trash.

At first he was not sure what it was. Was it plastic, did it belong to some mannequin or big doll? He touched it, picked it up, with curiosity turned it in his hands. . . . A human head—the head of a young woman. With a shrug of his shoulders he stuffed the globe in his bag and carried it home with him.

After taking off his jacket and pouring himself a glass of cheap vodka, he removed the head from his bag, placed it on his little table and cleaned it up with a damp rag.

He admired her features. She struck him as being incredibly beautiful and he wondered where she came from. Was she Ukrainian? Was she rich, was she poor? She had what he decided were sophisticated lips. Her hair was blonde. Her neck looked like it had been severed with a sharp instrument.

Later, while he was eating his supper of cabbage soup and kyshka, that sausage made from buckwheat and blood, he let his mind ramble. He wondered if she could speak, what she would say, if she would approve of him. Would she laugh, would she scream? Her presence touched him.

His life had had very little romance, but his emotions, though imbecile, were not without a certain hint of vitality—brought now into play by the sight of those stagnant, rolled back eyes, those wan cheeks and that rigid-proud chin.

That night he had trouble sleeping. The fact that a beautiful woman was so near him made him restless. When he awoke the next morning he was delighted to have her company. In the afternoon he smoked his pipe and talked to her . . . and she listened.

He fell deeply in love with that severed head of a woman.

He would run his coarse hand through the silky strands of her hair and murmur into her ears amorous words of longing. He would have liked to have taken her for a romantic walk, past Mariinskiy Palace, past St. Andrew's Cathedral, through the numerous city parks, to watch the lilacs and the chestnut trees bloom;— for spring was coming, the earth warming, grass was growing.

The thing began to corrupt: to stink and become infested with maggots. He was thus forced to keep it in the freezer, only removing it periodically for love making. One might have considered her to be not quite as beautiful like that—half corrupted, frozen—but he thought her more divine than ever. For hours on end he would stare into the thing's popping eyes, losing himself in their shiny, oozing splendour.

One day the landlord let himself in without knocking. The head was sitting on the table. Malevich quickly threw a rag over it and muttered a few disconnected, meaningless words. The landlord gloomily asked for the rent and left.

It was surely he who alerted the authorities, for the very next day they arrived and searched the premises.

The court psychiatrist declared that Malevich was mad. But it is easy to call a man in love a madman.

KINSHASA

IT is the Congo's largest city and a port on the Congo
River, which spreads before it, a vast expanse of water
on which overcrowded ferries float.

On the tropical landscape the city is a canker, a festering and open wound. Its centre is dominated by the
wide Boulevard du 30 Juin. In the shanty towns phaseurs
sleep on broken cardboard boxes and scavenge for food.
Lack of: electricity, running water, sewers, transport.

It is the Congo's largest city / ruled by kleptocracy.
It has over five million inhabitants. Maybe seven. Maybe more. Crowded: street children, traders, bare backs,
soldiers, smoke, slums. A city no one goes to without a
reason, no one goes to for enjoyment. Justice = a burning tire around the neck. Violence is a common way of
communication as are French and Lingala.

Her name is Bicha. She wears a bright-blonde wig.
She has a fine figure. In a white and tight jumpsuit. She
makes her way through the muddy alleys of the Cité.
Heaps of trash. Cement walls. Tin roofs. Hot and humid. Innumerable little shops. Women in dashikis. The

sun is setting. Pink. Egg-yolk orange. Now we see: paraffin lamps; the glow of cooking fires: people preparing food there in the open. Rice. Bitekuteku. Grilling fish. Laughter.

She makes her way into a dance bar. Music. Beer. Lights. White plastic tables. The latest version of Ndombolo. Many men: bootblacks, petty thieves, taxi-drivers, bacheques, vendors of diamonds and vendors of charcoal. Some spend their day's pay. Laughter. Some a month's wages. Many eyes turn towards her, many mouths want to chat her up; a few slatterns sneer. She dances with one man, she dances with another. Hands go up. Grab fistfuls of air. Winding of waists. Hands clap. Movement of hips. She bows her head, shakes suggestively, vigorously. Now a new partner: craving eyes, athletic build encased in an elegant, brightly-coloured outfit, capped with Turkish fez. He twists his legs, steps as if the floor were on fire; buttocks backward and forward; moves his body—a thing made of rubber—to the drums, to the diamond-sharp sound of the Almaz guitar. The concrete floor was wet with sweat.

"There is a room in back," he says.

"Take it."

Ten minutes later and they are there, lips pressed together, the music surging through the cinderblock walls. She is seductive, him mucronated. She detaches herself, drinks from her beer bottle. He drinks from his, finishes it. Arousal. She finishes hers; throws her bottle against the wall; throws his. Arousal. Glass scattered on the floor. He thinks she is frenetic, drunk, high.

"Don't be angry, my love," says he.

She grins.

Pause.

Pitcher of water by bedside. She dashes it on the floor. Shatter. Pause. She kisses him. Strips herself naked (magnificent display), throws herself down on the floor. Bicha lays there sprawling, a writhing blotch of skin, splinters of glass working their way into her back, behind.

"Come on," she cries, "what are you waiting for?"

Pause.

"I am your flesh dartboard!" she cries.

Her name is Bicha; desirous of perforation, to be hunted, empierced.

Her name is Bicha. She is attracted to sharp things. She drives needles into her cheeks, recklessly inserts them into her lips. She is a human pin-cushion. Deep-flesh insertions. She wants to be drilled into, punctured everywhere, through every square inch, be sewn to her lovers, gored on tusks. Cuspidate rutting. Sharp thorns tacks needles. Dress herself in barbed-wire. Wrapped up in beads of red. Copulate with knives, razors, spikes and spears. She goes with many men, scares them, when she insists on making love on broken glass, her dream to make love on a bed of nails. Make love to porcupine, pickaxe or scythe.

LONDON

"At Victoria Station. He acted very queer."

"That is because he is queer. —An odd one to be sure."

"You have known him for some time I take it?"

"We were at University together. —Not that we were particularly friends. —I don't know if he had any real friends."

"You did not care to be his friend?"

"I didn't care or not care. I was a healthy young man involved in other things. Cherwell was always a bit apart;—morose,—with his nose wedged between the pages of some French novel or other. *Spirite*—I remember seeing him read that. . . ." Durand took a sip of his wine. "After University, I didn't see the fellow for years," he continued. "Really I had forgotten about his existence altogether. . . . But then Miss Lolivrel. . . . I began to call on her . . ."

"And she is the one who introduced you to the séances," said Phillips.

"Yes, she did."

"I imagine you were surprised to see me there?"

"Well, I never took you for that sort of chap."

"I am not. It was Miss Gilbert's acquaintance I wished to cultivate, not that of the spirits."

Durand let out a short laugh. "I suppose most of the men there were like us. . . . But not Cherwell. . . . No, I am fully convinced that he believed all that tosh."

A short while later: outside. The two lit their pipes and began to make their way down Brewer Street, towards Regent Street.

"Speak of the . . ."

"Yes, that's him isn't it?"

"Do you think he's seen us?"

"Well, he's looking over now, isn't he?"

After faltering for a moment in indecision, Gerard Cherwell crossed over the street and approached. Greetings were exchanged.

"We seem to be running into each other quite often," Phillips said to Gerard, a thin, small man, with a black moustache and very pale skin.

"But I don't see you at Miss Gilbert's any more," said Gerard.

"I don't much go—I am not going there anymore."

"And you Durand? Have you—have you found something better also?"

"Better? . . . A glass of port and a volume of Macaulay is how I spend my Thursday evenings often enough."

"Oh, I thought that maybe you fellows had found something . . . *better?*"

"Well—and where are you off to?"

"Oh! I have to be going. Good evening!"

Gerard abruptly turned, up Bridle Lane, Marshall Street, towards Oxford Circus, towards Marylebone, his gait slow and careful. He passed pedestrians: a few rough looking fellows obviously just come from their pints; a woman, spicily dressed, living flesh to be had for coin of the realm. . . . Material flesh . . .

. . . Though there was a moon, it was faint. . . .

. . . Soon he was there, the street dark, unlit by gas jets . . . him now before a great old house of forbidding appearance, ominous, of ill-fame.

He went through the gate . . . took a latchkey from his pocket and opened the door, which creaked on its hinges. Inside, he lit a candle and stalked through the hallway, through the dining room, and into a small and gloomy back parlour. The furniture was old, much of it thick with dust. He set the candle down on a small table, unbuttoned his buff-coloured overcoat, and then sat down on the divan. One of his legs hooked itself over the next. He drew from his pocket a sachet, containing: life-everlasting flowers, henbane, dittany of Crete, and chicken bones, which he hung about his neck.

From his cigarette case, the rectangular top of which was decorated with an enamel plaque of Orpheus and Euridice, he extracted a cigarette, lit it; now looking at the ceiling, now the floor, to the right and left, a mixture of aromatic smoke and soft sighs escaping from his lips as he thought of those creatures who, in past times, must have inhabited this large house—this place once a den of vice and crime, of which at the present the neighbours complained of midnight howls and strange unearthly shrieks.

. . . Herbs, incense of tobacco (bait for whore); him now staring at the flame of candle . . .

A rapping sound was heard. His lips twisted into a peculiar smile. An unearthly chill swept over the room; and there was the tinkle of ghostly laughter. He felt himself touched by invisible hands. Slowly he pivoted on his buttocks, took up a couchant position.

"Yes," he murmured as the globes of eerie green light began to become manifest—to grow and open like morning-glories, out of the empty air, now joined by ghastly shapes, vague faces, figments of lust and sorrow—floating around him, beginning to diffuse about his person a silky white mist, ectoplasmic, softer than the softest virgin skin, more exciting than the hottest vitalic harlot.

. . . The girl beaten to death, but still up to her tricks. Soiled doves. The women who haunted, glided through, that once brothel, stew, house of prostitution, their faces thick with phantasmal paint, their howls exquisitely spine-tingling. . . .

Gerard shuddered. Ah! there really was nothing so exciting as licentious revelry with the spirits, with their creep!

LUXEMBOURG

" ALL men think they are great lovers," she murmured to herself as she walked along the battle-
ments, along the pedestrian promenade known as the
Chemin de la Corniche in that city set in the heart of
Europe. "But what a species! . . . Marcus, he has the stu-
pid gaze of an inhibited schoolboy . . . Pierre,—the man
smells like a goat . . . and Klaus, his tongue is too big to
fit in my mouth."

Veronica was pretty. She was tall, with somewhat large
hips and dark auburn hair; a skull rhombic and even;
rather dull brown eyes. She wore tight-fitting jeans and
a white cotton blouse; and made her way forward, into
the spectacular gorge, with arms crossed, shoulders ever
so slightly hunched, as if she were chilly, though it was a
warm, late afternoon of spring. . . . She was dreamy, her
thoughts on idealised love.

Bumpy. Dry. Toothless. She had been hearing it call
to her throughout those warm nights.

To the left: sheer descent; trees, in three or four shades
of green, rose up from below. The path was gradual and

pleasant. She passed by a pair of hikers and greeted them in Luxembourgish. They responded in French.

She continued down; and unfortunately encountered Klaus.

"Veronica!"

A healthy smile; symmetry of face; a man who would treat children and puppies well; with a well-developed chest and arms; a man who could only bring sadness to her flesh.

"Hello Klaus."

"I could love her," he thought; and then said: "Going for a walk?"

"Yes—I am walking down."

"I was going up, but . . ."

"It's so slow—and like a whale," she thought, eyeing his tongue; and then, with a shrug of her shoulders, said: "Okay, goodbye then."

"Call me sometime!"

She turned and walked away; in not a long while reached the bottom, cliffs and man-made walls pocked with casemate embrasures rising dramatically and high above her. To her right was the Pétrusse River, in front of her the twenty-four-arched Pont Viaduc which spanned the gorge.

There were pools of shade and bright-coloured flowers. The grass there below was exquisite. She strolled along, occasionally lifted a stone or piece of old wood and peered beneath. She sighed, pouted. "A beast," she thought, scanning the ground with her gaze. "Because of deep attraction. And I, a woman, have to look in strange places for pleasure—tactile pleasure." And then she saw what she was looking for. Huge, nearly as large as a dinner plate, it sat on the moist earth not far from a gurgling fountain.

Filled with excitement, she approached and kneeled near. It gazed at her with malicious and protruding eyes with vertically elliptical pupils, moved its short hind legs, took a few languid steps towards her. She touched its warty back with her swollen lips—its rump, its mouth—and then she reclined. It gulped down air, its vocal sac expanded, like a balloon, and the creature let out a long nasally trill of sound.

It now moved its batrachian feet. To her. Upon her. Up her thigh. Crawled (that amphibian of adventure) under her blouse. And she felt its weight. She felt its clammy skin against her flesh and shuddered.

There was nothing she liked more than to feel a toad creep across her belly; to witness its terre verte skin juxtaposed against her own, which was very white. And how often she dreamed of this lover, who fed on flies and worms, taking her, with its sticky tongue entwining her own, grasping her trunk with its forelimbs.

It clung to her, swallowed and blinked. She clenched her teeth, ground them together . . . in a paroxysm of pleasure.

MANILA

PRIMATE + muscle tissue + cow body.

Pollution smell incense overcrowded chaos prostitutes and faith healers fortune tellers and gules of deflowered meat barbecued innards wound grease-stained language of provoquant stitched-up screams.

Miss Fernandez. She lived in an enclosed mansion, a stone's throw away from poverty. Her agitation was always connected with meat meat = flesh + scent.

Sitting, back erect, in the cool of a vast air-conditioned room, she would be served. Half-raw beef; well-cooked pork. She ate monkey shish-kabobs and dogs, broiled crocodile and roasted house lizard. She would run her tongue over donkey meat, caress thick slabs of roasted horse.

(Dance eat devour snake neck stump bubbles with blood.)

She would pick up the flesh with her long thin fingers, supple as centipedes, plunge her teeth in, rip it shred it devour it. She gorged herself on water buffalo, stuffed her mouth full of sheep's brains.

Appetites awakened.

Occasionally she would leave the grounds of her mansion. As soon as she stepped outside the sweat began to course down her face, impearl her breasts. Then she would prowl, like some hungry animal, let her feet touch the dark sidewalks; passing by crumbling non-descript dwellings. And finding a young buck, she would lure him to some cheap hotel, where, enticing him with the fruits of heaven, she would plunge him into the seethe fires = seethe fires of hell char hell.

More often, she would remain at home, sending a servant (middle-aged woman with iron-coloured bun of hair) out to find some adequate fellow ready to earn a handful of pesos.

Rizal had a well-built body. He stood nervously before Miss Fernandez. She smiled, her sharp teeth glistened, her tongue, red as fire, caressing them hungrily.

She lavished him with goat meat; eating fried calf-livers, gazed into his eyes. She shoved pieces of half-cooked rare rare flesh into his mouth, kissed him as he chewed.

Like a blooded hound she grew frenzied, maddened; hurled herself upon the young man, wound her limbs around him like an octopus decapitated parlour game inspired fatty strands lust carabao + lips + murmur in liver sauce venado plunge wild loin.

In a carnivorous trance, she lashed the air with her hair. A croaking fever of turbulence carnassial hedonic alloy = tripe hung lingerie of sanguineous muck = 2 slice flesh beaten 2 meat piece bath of meat.

Exhausted, collapsed on a tiger-skin rug, she fell into the deepest of sleeps.

Two strong-armed servants entered. They grabbed the young man and expelled him onto the street—his belly full, heart empty.

MEXICO CITY

BROWN air. Businessmen, beggars, foreign tourists, street rodents, bodies against bodies in the depths of that great bowl of sophistication, pit of poverty. The city gurgled; trucks, spewing out black smoke, snorted along the streets.

Professor Carlos Villegas made his way through the suffocating crowd.

Sweltering summer lascivious weather. He, who rarely left the city even during holidays, was dressed in a loose and well-wrinkled seersucker suit. He was a thin and very tall man with a bushy moustache, a head of thick, shoulder-length black hair parted down the middle and green spectacles resting on a small, pointy nose. His face was heavily pockmarked. He was by no means hand-some—was in fact the very opposite. But behind those absolutely unappealing features a powerful brain was continuously at work. He was a genius; misunderstood and socially awkward.

Apparatus. Contrivance and function. Complex agency. A device that transmits. Breathing in air as thick as cheese, and brown as clay, he thought about slender string-like filaments of flexible metal rote memory monkey-do visual imitation smell chips servos.

He lit a cigarette and stalked down the stairs of the Juárez Station. A few moments later he was on Line 3, running south. The train rumbled along beneath the ground: shot along like electricity, like slow lightning.

He heard women gabbling together. A constant repetition of the five hundred most commonly used words in Spanish, delivered with unnecessary inflection.

"So emotional, these females," he murmured to himself.

At Balderas. People pour out. People pour in. He noted their hydraulics. Pneumatics. Beside him, below him now stood a pretty young lady. From his vantage point (by looking directly down) he could see the sweat-flecked brown skin of her bosom. He wondered what her coding system was like.

She looked up at him, as Empress Carlotta might have a louse found in her bedding at the Palacio Nacional. Her lips curled in disdain. She moved away from him, human lizard, in instinctive repulsion. He shrugged his shoulders, with the thumb and forefinger of his right hand smoothed his moustaches, which were as unruly, as impossible to tame as two half-starved jaguars. Indeed, he was well used to this reaction from members of the opposite sex. But what did it matter? He had better at home.

He de-boarded at Zapata. Was soon above ground. He made his way along the sidewalks, crossed the street, dodged through traffic, entered his building, climbed the stairs. His apartment was a disaster, books, beer bottles, wires, tools strewn in disorder. There was an unpleasant odour. Cockroach traps lined the baseboards.

He took off his jacket and loosened his tie.

"Paulina, I'm home!"

A faint whirring.

"Carlos."

He walked into the small, dark bedroom.

A beautiful woman sat on the unmade bed. She was attired in a flimsy négligée. Breasts like strawberries floating in bowls of milk. Her appearance was certainly at odds with her surroundings.

She stared at Carlos blankly.

"Welcome back Carlos," she said in a sweet, but somewhat stilted voice.

She was absolutely unemotional, and that is what Carlos liked, as the only emotions women ever felt for him were negative.

He touched her cold skin, squeezed her rubbery flesh.

"You like that, Paulina?" he asked.

"Carlos," she said. "Yes. Carlos."

She was as flexible as an insect, as resilient as a rhinoceros. He removed his spectacles and sat down next to her, kissed the oil from her lips.

She was motionless.

He became more ardent. His right hand became like Amerigo Vespucci, his left like Nuñez de Balboa (valiant explorers).

She was motionless.

Somewhat agitated, he pursed his lips and rose from her side.

"Silly little problem," he murmured.

He took the cord that projected from her spine, like some bizarre tail, and plugged it into the wall. A slow whirring sound came from the machine. It bat its eyelids. Trembled. One hundred billion neurons in motion capable of one hundred trillion connections. The lithe wriggling of servo-pneumatic muscles as the speech synthesizer activated.

"009889 . . . 009890 . . . 009891 . . . Carlos. Yes. Carlos. Kiss me. Carlos. Mating mating mating."

"Ah," Professor Villegas murmured, caressing her chin, that lump of electroactive polymers, "it seems even you have problems from time to time."

MOSCOW

"HE was hanging in your bedroom from a meat-hook."

"Yes."

"You murdered him."

"I did not."

"Who hung him there?"

"I did."

"Parts of him were missing."

"Yes."

"What do you know about that?"

"I ate him."

Silence in the court.

"You ate him but did not murder him?"

"I ate him."

"Do you often eat people?"

"He wanted me to eat him. We corresponded. He came to my house and I ate him."

"You corresponded?"

"I advertised in the *Novoye Vremya* and he answered. I wanted to eat someone and he wanted to be eaten. We met at the Ferris wheel at Gorky Park. He was very nice and we got along well. We walked and had coffee together and then I took him up to my apartment."

"And you murdered him."

"No. I cut off one of his fingers. This one . . . the thumb. He bled a lot but it was good. I fried it in oil and ate it."

"He did not mind?"

"No. He wanted to try. I cut off four more of his fingers and he ate two and I ate two. . . . It was very nice. It felt very, very nice."

"And then?"

"We drank vodka. He did not feel well and lay on the couch. We listened to the radio and talked. He worked at a record shop in the Noginsk district. He said he knew English and some French. He said that he was happy to have met me."

"So you could eat him?"

"Yes. I cut off his arm and put it in the oven. When I pulled out his entrails they smelled very nice. I wanted to chop him all up. I cut off his left leg but did not eat it."

"He was dead?"

"Not when I ate his arm. I offered him some, and he took a bite but was very weak. He enjoyed it though."

"You murdered him."

"I ate him. It made us feel very good."

"You murdered him."

"I ate him."

NEW YORK

A MAGGOT heap millions strong a beast of glass and steel black pollutants pus. Taxis buzz bees on asphalt steaming miasma eyes masks not just for faces a city that wakes up early goes to bed late at night a great bed of burning coals.

––––––––

Stimulation.

––––––––

Towers and trains F to Brooklyn 7 to Queens 1 to Bronx 242 St. He lived in Midtown, near the 4, 5 and 6 lines / trainwheel sparks.

––––––––

Stimulation.

––––––––

Alex was into energy energy liked the flow of currents. He looked at the lights. Looked at the lights / Times Square Madison Broadway Garden.

"It's the charges I like. Electricity. That's what powers this whole place. As a child they told me not to do it. I did it. That was when feelings first awoke in me."

He had a head small enough to be called microcephallic. A scanty moustache and beard; a thin nose; (eyeglasses); a sunken chest below which protruded a soft bubble of a belly.

———————

"I sometimes wonder what she would look like if she had a body. White hot. The trembling lines of her figure. Shock me. Riding through my very bones. Shock me [electromotive breasts force flowing mane motion charged thigh particles lips high amperage galvanic eyes cells]."

———————

The static of carnal kisses did not effect his wearying flesh; and he craved jolts. The static of human = too low a voltage. He wanted the electricity of the entire city coursing-throbbing through him. Jaded jaded each day requiring stronger stimulation / violet wand / transcutaneous electronic neurological stimulator / plasma globe / cattle prod.

———————

He would wander the great corridors of the city, look at its symbols.
Ah ah ah ah ah.

———————

Tingle.

———————

Electrical stimulation.
Edge play.

———————

It was a hot July day. He gazed at the large fish tank, at the snake-like electric eel winding slowly therein. . . . But that was not fervent enough for him. . . . Electric catfish, aba-aba, black ghost fish: he had tried them all. . . .

He fingered the Terminator 2 advanced electronic anti-barking collar. . . . But he already knew its twenty-fourth level far too well.

Need for stronger stimulant. Need for stronger stimulant. Cut plug from air conditioner. Caress wire. Strip end of wire naked. Strip end of wire naked. Caress naked wire. Naked. Plug in. Pause. Naked. Touch. Tzzzkk! Touch. Tzzzkk! Toes. Calves. Zzzkk! Heating of body tissue. . . . Burn. . . . Then: Tzzzkk! Hold. Tzzzkk! Passion. Hold. Tzzzzkk! Hold. Burn. Tzzzzzckkk! Passion. Burn. Zzzzzzckckk! Passion. Muscular contraction. . . . Passion . . . . Burn. . . . Beyond . . . let go . . . threshold. . . . And he . . . could not . . . let go. . . . . . . (Electrical / obsession). . . . . . . Zzzck! Zzzck! Zzzck! . . . . . . Ffffsssz-zzckhkhkh!

OSLO

IT was summer. The sky was of an extraordinary blue. The days were very long.

The two men, one old, one young, walked along Karl Johan Street, from the direction of the Royal Palace.

The elder man, Harald Bjørgen, impeccably dressed, and of a somewhat grave and upright bearing, put his arm through that of the younger.

"You need not get so carried away by these matters Christoffer," he said. "You are enraptured by sentiments, but sentiments are even more ephemeral than a woman's body which, like other fruits, is only good for a season."

"Then you consider love to be preposterous?"

Bjørgen gently stroked the wings of his moustache. "Not preposterous," he said, "but certainly a hindrance to pleasure."

"Then there is no pleasure in love?"

"No. There is only pleasure in being loved."

"But that is mad! If such were the case, then all you have taught me would be . . ."

The words died on Christoffer's lips.

Bjørgen smiled. "My dear fellow, I said there was no pleasure in loving. I said no such thing about *making love*."

"But then why, when I speak of her eyes, and the rotundity of her breasts, do you look on me as if I were a puppy?"

"Every great libertine starts out as a puppy. It is a prerequisite for becoming a hound. When I was a young man, I too thought as you do. I was shallow-minded and thought the stimulation produced by touching a woman's hams to be the very Olympus of luxury. But refined libertinism, like a refined taste for wine, is a thing gained over time; learned, as a great athlete learns to ski, to soar like a bird above the spectators' heads, to hazard down treacherous slopes at breathtaking speed. . . . Yes, one is not born a Birger Ruud of the bedroom."

They passed cafés, the outdoor tables full of people. The scene was a juxtaposition of vibrant primary colours, reminiscent of an Edvard Munch painting; wide eyes and pasty oval faces were in accord.

Bjørgen put his hand lightly on his protégé's shoulder. "Ah, you are still young and have yet to learn of the subtleties of gyneolatry—have yet to fathom where the jewels of a woman's body lie." His white teeth flashed as he spoke, pronouncing his words with the clear precision of a pedagogue. "The art of pleasing oneself consists in arriving at a woman's most delectable harbour."

"I can guess where that is."

"Can you though? . . . Hmmm. . . . Those piquant nests of curly golden down . . . and their aroma, that pleasurable animal stench that sends quivers coursing down a healthy man's spine. Indeed, what pleasure could be greater than to bury one's nose in that soft fleshy envelope, have it be tickled by those feminine filaments, and breathe deeply, breathing in that nocturnal odour of dilection—blondes with their scent of carnal gold—brunettes, the hot delight of roasted chestnuts. . . . And then . . . and then the redhead, the finest of all, bright orange flames flickering, shooting forth from the pits of her arms—an aroma of curry leaves, a spicy delicacy, a humid garden in which to lose one's very senses!"

He was visibly moved. His lips quivered as he spoke.

He took a monographed platinum cigarette case from his jacket pocket, extracted a cigarette, and lit it, inhaling deeply.

"Only when a man's taste becomes thoroughly refined in the crucible of romantic experience, can he truly appreciate the magic of the axilla, where the desires of the animal merge with the pleasure of the deity. A woman's smell, gamy as a hunted fox, is the igniter of memories and passions. To inhale it is to inhale her most secret substance. That tangle of hair, that undiscovered country is, in truth, more intimate than her very soul and I would cast myself into, merge with it as salt does with water, not denying it a single particle of my being!"

"And . . . shaved?" the young man ventured.

"Ah, this modern infatuation with shaving," Bjørgen replied with disdain. "It might well be the ruin of the human race. . . . It is all the fault of the Americans, with their gross and misguided sense of hygiene."

The two men continued in silence, each deep in thought. They passed book-sellers and plate-glass windows which reflected their own images—uncertain, quaking stripes of pink and black. Trolley cars hummed past them. And above lurched that formidable pasture of molten sky.

Presently, simultaneously, they raised their eyes.

A young woman, dressed in jeans and a candid tank top, was walking towards them. A mass of golden-brown hair spilled from her cranium. She was pretty, with a small nose and huge mouth. When she was just by them, Bjørgen slightly inclined his head.

"Excuse me miss," he murmured, "but do you have the time?"

Her elbow rose until it became vertical with her shoulder.

"It is twenty-two minutes past two," she said in a mellow cadence.

"Thank you."

The woman continued on her way.

Christoffer smiled. "Very clever," he said, pointing to the gold watch wrapped around Bjørgen's wrist, "considering that you have a punctual time-piece at your disposal."

"I knew it and she knew it both. But the woman does not exist who will not flaunt her apocrine glands when asked."

PARIS

" A RE you free?" he drawled.
He wore a tightly-buttoned grey frock coat. Creased trousers. An ascot tie. Kid skin gloves, the right wrapped around a bone-handled cane. His head was mounted by a great shiny silk hat, like a chimney, and his moustaches glistened. . . . Obviously an aesthete, the sort of fellow who spent a pair of hours every day before his altar, his toilette table. . . . And a craving glint in his eye that she well knew. . . .

The rain had stopped some thirty minutes before and the woman was there; on the Place Blanche at the foot of Montmartre; one of the first on the street in the late afternoon; thirsty for money. . . . She was somewhat down at one-strap Grecians with a standard Louis heel, her person ever so slightly ragged.

She said that she was free; sincerely hoped to exploit this rich-looking gentleman who now motioned her to follow him.

Mono-bosomed, with a long-waisted torso, one hand held a folded absinthe-coloured umbrella fringed with lace. Puffed sleeves and dangle earrings. A choker, a simulated pearl dog collar encircled her throat and her arms were sheathed in full-length, red satin gloves. She had cunning little eyes which peeped out from a pretty though fatigued face, heavily powdered; and then, perched on top of a soft pile of Pompadour hair, was an outrageous hat, from which a worn-looking ostrich plume vibrated.

Without the slightest attempt at conversation, he led her: some blocks away: to a shoe store: which together they entered.

A show clerk approached.

"Yes, Monsieur, how may I help you?"

"This young lady is in need of a pair of shoes—the most expensive pair of shoes you have."

The man looked her up and down, raised his eyebrows, pursed his fat lips together.

"She has small feet."

"Yes, she does."

Thirty minutes later the gentleman and woman exited the shop. She stepped gingerly: pointed toes and heels, as fine as a pin, with a scalloped top.

"Now walk there. . . . Yes, there . . . in the street."

"It is wet."

"Be a good girl. . . . Step in the puddle."

She shrugged her shoulders, an experienced streetwalker, did as she was told.

He had her trudge through the gutter, place her feet in mud and fresh manure;—then to the Rue des Abbesses, where St. Denis had been beheaded, to the Rue Marcadet and even a tour through the Cité de Naples, where her pretty footwear came in contact with, was splattered by, the refuse and spit of every human vice, the area pervaded by the stench of festering sewage and rotting poverty. He watched her disgusting promenade with composure. She became tired, irritable.

. . . When they reached more comfortable streets, in the dying light of day, he summoned her to him, to the sidewalk, then had her step against the side of a butcher shop, somewhat out of public view. He flung himself on his knees before her. His hat fell from his head. He grovelled; set his lips to the shoes;—next tongue: lapping at and licking the leather,—moans and sighs,—all the signs of a man experiencing the greatest pleasure,—licking it until it shone.

He then rose to his feet, picked up his hat and placed it on his head, brushed off his trousers and removed his wallet from his pocket. He handed the woman a twenty-franc note and then turned and walked away, dabbing at his mouth with a handkerchief as he went.

That evening it turned windy.

PEKING

PRINCE ZHU was the eldest son of Qiyu, the Jingtai Emperor.

He had a very round face and a fine chin out of which sprouted the tiniest filament of a beard. His lips were as red as cherries and his skin white as rice-flour. He had lovely eyes. Though he was delicate, he was strong. Skilled in the use of the mace, he could have slaughtered a dragon. He knew his books and wrote very pretty poetry.

Indeed he was an exceptional young man.

He had a passion for beautiful things: calligraphy and painting. But most especially he liked ceramics, on which he expended a large portion of his allowance. He had Banshan period pots, Han and Tang dynasty figures and white wares from Ding Shou. He refreshed himself sometimes from Yue kiln tea sets with their striking watery-blue glaze; while at others he used cups from the Lungquan kiln, with a glaze so thin as to be translucent; while the leaves themselves were kept in a shadow-blue glaze tea caddy.

His collection was indeed remarkable. There was an egg-white glazed bowl from Hutian Village; a hollyhock-shaped flower pot with a rose-purple glaze; a Han earthenware dog with an elongated neck; a late Yangshao urn; a horse with a sancai glaze with bridle and decorative medallions separately cast. He had countless vessels, plates and figurines of every sort.

But his most prized possession was a jar said to have come from the Ru kiln. Yet it was so large, of such divine beauty, the prince suspected that it more likely was made by some heavenly immortal. It had a thick, crackled greyish-blue, almost lavender glaze which gave it the appearance of polished jade. The fine support marks on its base resembled sesame seeds. Its shape was exquisitely feminine, graceful and light; so much so that the prince could not resist.

The emperor sat in the Western Study, but could not enjoy his spring wine.

"You wish to marry a vase?" he said gravely. "I don't see the advantage of such an alliance."

"But I love her."

"A man's life should be regulated by nature."

"In the great boundlessness, all is nature."

Later, that evening, the emperor summoned his chief eunuch Wang to him. The latter approached and bowed twice. The emperor, with an air of sadness, told him of his son's request.

"To submit to his wish would be madness," Wang said. "To refuse it would be perilous. Heaven has its periods of spring and autumn, winter and summer. In spring one tills the soil, in autumn one brings in the harvest. In summer we relax in the shade, in winter we warm ourselves near the brazier. I suggest you humour the prince."

"How?"

"Let him think he has married the vase. Later, when his mind clears, you can reveal the truth. He will be grateful and be ready to marry any mortal woman of your choosing."

Though the family objected to the marriage, they went through with the ceremony all the same—thinking it was best, for the time being, to comply with the young man's mood in order to soothe him, as surely later he would awake from his folly.

The prince spent his time enclosed in the Eastern Chamber, alone with the porcelain vase. Sometimes the sound of his jade flute could be heard, sometimes the sound of his sweet singing—the words carrying with them a passion deeper than any pool.

When he went out, he would have the vase carried in a palanquin just behind him, as if indeed it were his royal consort; sometimes taking his beloved to Accumulated Beauty Hill to enjoy the scenery, sometimes to Angler's Terrace to sit beneath the weeping willows.

At night, when the emperor visited the Hall of Earthly Tranquillity, his wife, instead of applying herself to his conjugal wishes, would shed tears on his shoulder.

A rumour spread through the city that the prince was mad.

Was this the way for the heir apparent to behave?

The emperor summoned Wang to him.

"A year ago," he said in an agitated voice, "I asked your advice. You spoke of summer, winter, autumn and spring, advising patience. But the four seasons have come and gone without in the least diminishing my son's infatuation with the vase. On the contrary, he seems more in love than ever, and I am weary of being bathed at night in the tears of the empress."

"Your Highness, remember," Wang advised, "that the straight tree is the first to be cut down, so a little peccadillo should not be excessively fretted over. To me it seems the prince is in every way a great man. Where the cliffs rise highest, white clouds amass. His only fault lies in this bizarre infatuation he has for the Ru kiln vase. It is my opinion that if the vase were taken away from him, his problem would cease."

"But he would never tolerate this."

"As the ancients say: 'He who anticipates difficulties, never encounters them.' . . . The prince need not know."

The chief eunuch then approached the emperor and whispered his plan into his ear.

It was the third watch of the subsequent night.

Two palace guards had been given the task. They were big, formidable looking men with bushy beards.

They removed their eight-laced shoes and entered the prince's private chambers in silence, walking on the tips of their toes over the embroidered mats.

"I don't see him."

"All the better, here's the vase."

They rolled up their sleeves and set about removing the object.

"Not light is it?"

"Hey, for twenty strings of cash I could carry one in each hand!"

They tied a hempen cord around the object, attached it to a bamboo pole, and carried it off between them. They left the Palace of Heavenly Purity and made their way to the West Flowery Gate.

Once out of the Purple Forbidden City, they walked with brisk, swaggering steps through the large, orderly streets of the city proper, which were completely empty at that hour due to the curfew.

They traversed the Great City Street, passed the Temple of Heaven, and went through the Southern Gate, showing the gate-keeper their royal pass.

Some short distance from the thick city walls there was a gorge, over which a bridge passed.

The men arrived at the bridge just as butterfly wings began to dust the peony's red petals.

They heaved the vase up. Below a thin stream ran amongst numerous egg-shaped stones.

"Did you hear something?"

"Birds."

"No, from the vase."

"Nonsense. Over the side it goes!"

The vessel fell down into the bottom of the ravine, was shattered to shards and dust. A tree can shed its leaves before they are yellow; rain can come before the clouds have formed. The prince had been sleeping inside his beloved's womb and now lay there a lump of twisted skin and broken bones. The shards of the vase had pierced his flesh and heart and his blood ran over the stones and mixed with the water.

The two servants flew for their lives, the chief eunuch was beheaded, the queen's hair turned white. The sorrow of the emperor was profound.

QUITO

OSWALDO CORNEJO TOBAR walked slowly through the Plaza de la Independencia, a cigarette dangling from his thick lips, which sat like two mating slugs, slimy and elongated, beneath the thick bush of his moustache. The day was quite warm. He had the appearance of one bored: sleepy eyes, slow, dragging steps. Like a man digesting a big lunch.

His relationship with Elena was becoming decidedly uninteresting.

He seemed to have grown tired of her.

She wept. He yawned.

It was obvious that they would not be together for much longer.

Ah, why is it that such beautiful things can come to an end!

He remembered when they had first met. At the beginning she hadn't struck him as anything special. She was pretty, but . . .

A few kisses. Some hand-holding.

He certainly wasn't enthusiastic.

And then, one day, she was hit by a bus. Her left leg was broken in two places and set in a cast. Oswaldo became suddenly more tender, attentive. Their love life was abruptly filled with fresh riches.

He visited her every day, brought her flowers and candy, showered her brow, lips and breasts with a rain of tropical kisses.

As the sun began to set, he would take her out in her wheel chair. He would guide her through the streets and along park paths, occasionally sinking his nose into her forest of black hair, occasionally planting a kiss on her warm and slender neck.

Talk about romance!

But then, when the initial swelling went down, the plaster cast was exchanged for a lighter-weight fibreglass one.

He grew moody when she talked about finally taking it off.

"Let's change the subject," he said.

"But I can't stay with a cast on forever."

"Let's change the subject, please!"

Her leg was already healed. The doctor told her it was time to have it removed. She missed appointment after appointment.

"Oswaldo," she sniffed, "I just don't understand . . ."

He took her by the hand. "Listen," he murmured. "Your left leg is getting better. . . . Okay, I can see that. So, fine—you want to go to the doctor. But look, my love . . ."

"Oh, so you do still love me!"

"Of course I do! Don't talk such damned nonsense. I love you so much it hurts. But you have to understand. I need a certain fragility in a woman. . . . You know, a relationship is about give and take. . . . Your left leg is healed. Okay. . . . Let's develop this thing. Work with it. . . . We could break your right leg, and maybe an arm too—you would look nice like that!"

She stood frozen for a moment, staring at him with wide eyes.

"Oswaldo!"

And then her lips curdled. Huge tears leaped from her eyes.

"Ah, dammit!" he cried and stormed out of the house.

He walked slowly through the Plaza de la Independencia, a cigarette dangling from his thick lips. The day was quite warm. Sticky. A shoeshine boy approached him. A girl leaning against a lamp-post winked at him. He ignored them both. Ugly things.

Life seemed a pretty grim business. Dreary. When a man is asked to sacrifice his dreams . . .

Old loves wither and die. But fresh ones always bloom.

The cigarette went erect in his mouth. His sleepy eyes awoke. He inhaled deeply, then took the cylinder and flicked it to the ground.

His vision was magnetised to: a young woman, maybe twenty-three, maybe twenty-four, simply dressed, yet not without dignity. Her figure was a little too plump, her face a little too plain. But hey! She walked with crutches. A white cast protruded from beneath the hem-line of her dress.

The temperature of a sudden became quite tolerable. The sky seemed a little bluer. The people less hideous. His steps became more elastic. He followed the crutching woman through the crowd, taking in every one of her struggling movements with delight.

"What a mysterious creature," he thought.

On the Plaza de San Francisco she stopped to buy an apple from an Indian woman.

It was then that Oswaldo Cornejo Tobar approached her.

"Excuse me, but . . ."

"Who are you?"

"I saw you walking."

"Did you want me to fly?"

"I saw you walking—really having a hard time—and . . ."

She was wiping the apple on her shirt. She looked somewhat frightened.

"What do you want?"

"You see, you are such a beautiful young woman. And I am far from bold."

"You don't seem so shy."

"I had to talk to you. I couldn't let you get away."

"Well . . . you can talk."

"If I could offer you a drink?"

"You move quickly!"

Yes, once fired with enthusiasm, Oswaldo lost no time. Within an hour he had signed her cast, drawn a heart upon it.

And, from signing a woman's cast, to other things, is only a short distance.

He felt once again that his life had meaning. He nursed his new found love with a thousand caresses, fed her off the thick passion of his lips. Again, the world was painted in bright shades of ecstasy. The moon was a giant pearl. The girl's eyes dual oceans of unmatched profundity. He would bury his head in her breast, let his hand gently stroke her plaster. He filed down the rough spots with an emery board, elevated the leg with pillows. On washing days, he tied a plastic bag around her leg and guided her to the shower.

Never mind that she smelled slightly of onions. He loved her!

Loved! . . .

Until that fateful day when . . .

Yes, legs heal.

Oswaldo Cornejo Tobar disappeared from her life, without explanation, without useless goodbyes.

Later, dressed in his best suit, he would haunt the vicinity of the Hospital Metropolitano. Women with neck-braces, fibreglass arm cylinder casts and minervas were all within his scope. Like some deranged bee, he went from one broken flower to the next.

Sometimes he would have a passing fling with a woman with a sprained wrist or ankle. But his greatest passion he reserved for those whose legs were entombed in weighty casts—the result of complete comminuted compound fractures—those prostrated beings who had need of a man to help remove their itching.

Casts, in many shapes and sizes. These were the delights of Quito.

ROME

A GROUP of rich men convened together. They lay on couches arranged around low tables. They drank and they ate.

"My wife has got herself a lover," one man said. "An ex-gladiator. An Egyptian with powerful shanks."

"My wife's lover is a poet."

"Mine has a Greek slave who she keeps perfumed."

"The lover of my wife," a certain wealthy merchant by the name of Labrax said, "is kept in a pool in our courtyard."

"Charming."

"It is an octopus, with eight muscular arms, each one designed for love."

"Well, a happy wife means a happy husband," said a certain senator, rolling a grape languidly between his plump fingers.

SEVILLE

DON IGNACIO YÁNEZ DE MIRANDA was one of the best duellists of his age. A small, pale-faced man—he was elegant in his attire, haughty, as dangerous as a hornet. By the time he was thirty-three years old, he had killed seventeen men, broken the tips off half a dozen swords. It was then that he purchased an Alonso Perez blade—a beautiful item, long and sleek. It had a silver-plated hilt, which consisted of two large arms, a diagonal side-ring running from the forward end of the quillon-block to the bottom of the rear arm, a pair of loop-guards joined in the centre by a grooved block, and two projecting bars curving up from the bottom of the arms towards the pommel—which was forked, faceted and heat-shrunk onto the tang. The grip was wire-wrapped. The whole had a dramatic, decidedly elegant look to it.

But in spite of all this beauty, Don Ignacio was not convinced.

"Many men," he told himself, "have been run through while holding a fashionable sword in their hand."

A few days after the above mentioned purchase, Don Ignacio was riding his palomino—a beautiful, hawk-profiled animal bred at the Carthusian monastery—through the market. He saw an acquaintance of his whom he had not seen for a number of years and dismounted. The two men were talking and laughing together when they were startled by an abrupt neighing and the commotion of hooves. Don Ignacio turned and saw a man abusing his horse. In a formidable tone of voice, he requested the man to desist.

"Is this your nag then?" the other said. "Well—the damned thing has stepped on my foot—might have broken my toe—certainly ruined a fine pair of boots! A horse of an ass I would call it!"

Don Ignacio became even paler than usual.

"You have insulted me," he said.

"I have"

And so a duel was arranged.

"Do you know who you were just arguing with?" Don Ignacio's friend asked him.

"I do. It was Lorenzo de la Flores Zapoteca."

"Yes—a disciple of Don Luis Pacheco de Narváez. A deadly swordsman."

"So I have heard," Don Ignacio said carelessly.

The truth of the matter however was that he was concerned. The man he was up against was formidable, and he cursed the fact that he had to go up against him with a new, as yet untested blade. To him it seemed like a stroke of bad luck. All duellists are superstitious.

They met early the next morning in a field at the edge of town. Don Lorenzo cut the air with his blade and advanced with confidence. Don Ignacio met the oncoming attack skilfully. The two compassed for a time, steel whistled and rang against steel. Then of a sudden Don Lorenzo, biting his bottom lip, delivered a rather subtle *mandoble* which left Don Ignacio with a bleeding cut on his face. The latter was agitated, indebted, and quickly returned the favour by running the man through. He was somewhat surprised at how easily the sword slid between the man's ribs, through the man's body, as if the latter were nothing more than some great lump of soft cheese.

"Ah," he murmured wiping the blood from the blade, "it seems that you have passion as well as beauty."

He became a veritable hunter, prowling the streets of the city in search of human game. He would take offence at anything—an unfriendly look, a man knocking against him in a crowd—and, if apologies were not forthcoming, he would, with a feeling of great inner joy, demand satisfaction.

In duels it leapt about wickedly, always seemed eager to taste of other men's blood—was indeed a flirtatious piece of metal. With it he killed a man under the orange trees of the Girlada, and cut another to ribbons by the Monasterio de Santa Maria de Las Cuevas. When walking down the street with her at his side, he felt enormous pride. He loved to dance with her, to see her body flash through the air.

He delighted in removing it from its sheath and admiring its sleek and sensual form. He drilled constantly. In the courtyard of his house the sword could be heard singing from morning to night. When the weather was bad, he would sit in his parlour, flexing his fingers and gazing dreamily at the gleaming blade. Her figure was lithe, attractive in the extreme. She was hard and sharp; flexible and strong—with a heart of sweet steel.

"Ah, you coquette!" he would murmur to himself.

When he kissed her she poked him, when he hugged her she cut him. It was frustrating to have a lover so sharp, a lover so cold.

Indeed, she always seemed to be lunging after other men, never quite giving herself body and soul to him.

His friends commented on the fact that he had begun to keep so much to himself. He seemed to only derive pleasure from duelling, from the spilling of blood. He gained the reputation of an eccentric.

One evening, after attending mass at Iglesia de San Julián, Don Ignacio returned home and, stripping his sword from her sheath, so she stood naked, addressed her thus:

"I have prayed to God and the Virgin de la Hiniesta to show me a way," he said. "My heart burns with the most ardent love for you, but you subtly shun me, and fate seems to have willed it for my great desire to go unfulfilled." His eyes glowed in their dark sockets and his lips trembled as he continued: "I have prayed for mercy, for this great sin I am about to commit to be washed clean in the light of the after life! . . . My love!"

He plunged her into his heart, joyful to finally feel the cold steel puncture his breast.

SYBARIS

OPULENT. City of extravagance, leisure. The roofs
of the houses were extended so the streets were
always in shade and, where there were no houses, trees
were planted to provide shade. Sleep, eat and love. In
rooms lavishly furnished. The population was addicted
to luxury, provided with cooks and jesters and dancers
obscene. No Hellenic city could compare with its wealth,
magnificence.

It was said that Onomarchus had the most refined
senses. He slept on a bed of rose petals. Sometimes he
would have his pillows stuffed with basil, sometimes with
lavender. He would have his slaves doused in oil of dill.

The smell of ripe apples excited him to the highest pitch and in the fall, when the orchards were full, he
would lay in their midst with his nostrils distended wide.

Sometimes, when he was feeling particularly naughty,
he would ask for goats to be led into his parlour, for their
odour was that of love and (animals aside) he judged
women, not by how they looked, but by how they smelled.

For what met the eye meant nothing to him who cared only for that which met the nose—joining his beloved on a pile of black pepper, where they could roll together, while slaves burnt cloves and caraway and fanned in the fragrance of freshly chopped onions.

SYDNEY

THE softest things are often prone to disturb the senses the most violently; and nerves are made up of memories, reflections, hidden breaths, like feathers, around which smiling and moveable lids of skin close.

Spongy. Supple. Like so many gargoyles, turned from stone into undemanding furry fabric.

There were many of them there and her eyes traced over the form of each: the eighteen-inch-high kangaroo, in brown and white, the koala, truly adorable, the ostrich with its appealing beak. . . . Finally she found her choice: a kiwi, a thing indeed that seemed as if it had been made to give love, cuddly in the extreme.

"He's a cute one, isn't he?" the woman at the cash register commented.

Sabatha smiled enthusiastically, happy to know that there were others like-minded.

She left the shop, took it out of its bag and looked at it, felt its fur. A man with a flat nose looked at her. Well, maybe it was funny, a grown girl like her with a fuzzy thing like that. But better to feel the fuzzy than kiss a hammer.

Oh, she was not naïve, not totally naïve. She had, after all, been to King's Cross, walked along Darlington Road, under the neon lights, seen the things that begged to be seen. And she had known men—enough of them—there were always plenty of men to know—or never know—or ignore and brush aside.

Because there were the others.

Her house was filled with them: lined up on shelves, placed upon the couch, the chairs—and of course, many in her bed.

She often fantasised about being taken by a stuffed bear, ravished by a plush tiger.

Fleeciness. Huggability. And she enjoyed dressing them up in bondage gear, kept them constantly cologned—an echidna thick with grey hair and animal glove puppets. She ran her index finger along the centre seam of a pink elephant with white inside ears and sewn eyes, pushed her lips against an adorable prong-horned antelope and fell asleep next to Jeremiah, the fuzzy green frog.

No, her stuffed animals would never lie to her or leave her, never betray her or break her tender heart.

THEBES

USERMAATRESETEPENRE, King of Egypt, was thoroughly infatuated with noses. To him they were the most beautiful of all things; at night, he dreamed about making love to them.

He found women with large nostrils especially attractive, and relished in the extreme the sight of those round holes, resembling the mouths of famished beasts, as they dilated and quivered. At times he enjoyed indulging himself in a long and pointy organ of smell which, when well oiled, would glisten in the lamplight like a naked and dangerous sword. Yet, in the shifting sands of his moods, certain days arrived when for him satisfaction could only be procured by wrapping his lips around some nose swollen and gibbous, one endowed with substantial flesh.

During the hot afternoons of summer he would recline on a couch of gold, sipping at a goblet of pale and aromatic Taeniotic wine, and watch a favourite slave girl from Lebanon named Iniihue. That part of her face above her mouth was greatly extended, of ample proportion, a veritable cucumber; and she would come before him and move her body to the strains of the sistrum,—the instrument's sound reminiscent of a breeze cutting briskly through papyrus reeds. He had another girl from Nubia, endowed with a grand snub, which he took great pleasure in tweaking, in twisting between his own agile fingers. Then there were others, a whole harem of them, gathered from all parts of the known world, and daily they would be led out, each fitted with a big nose ring, each attached to the next by means of a long chain of electrum. So many exotic beaks! Some aquiline, others broad and beautiful, saddle-shaped.

The walls of his palace were painted with fantastical figures, women so mythically gifted that they needed an entourage of two dozen men pacing before them in stoic profile in order to carry that precious organ;—then noses in the shape of palm trees, serpents and fruits;—consistently outrageous: a proboscis long and supple as that of an elephant; another proud as that of the camel. And his sculptors, each one trying to outdo the next, carved for him giant and perfectly proportioned noses out of the finest granite and marble, while other artisans depicted them wonderfully in ivory and ebony—on wig boxes and cosmetic chests;—and then there were nose-shaped vessels of alabaster.

Insatiable, curious, always up for some fresh adventure, he would leave his palace in disguise, and drive through and around the great city on his chariot, past all of its one hundred gates, in search of women with unusual or prominent convexities on their faces. One day, while passing along the Street of the Weavers, he caught sight of a maiden possessed of an object highly attractive and cornute. Enticed, he subdued her, dragged her back home to his private apartments, and spent the following week lost in the great garden of her charms. Another time he saw, right beside one of the Colossi of Memnon, a beggar woman whose nose was as pronounced as one of the Libyan Hills;—and, bestowing upon her the gift of his lust, he lifted her out of poverty and placed her in a position of concubinage.

. . . He floated up and down the Nile on his golden barge. He sampled women with noses like stars, females with noses like moons.

It was after the Festival of Opet, that the king, that source of well-being for all Egypt, complained to his steward, Nkuku.

"Of ornaments of the other sex," he said, "I know much—have experienced many. But not one worthy to sit beside me on the throne."

"Usermaatresetepenre, Born of Re, Father of Amun, God Ruler of Iunu, what is the quality you most look for in your future bride?"

The king shrugged his shoulders, frowned, was taken aback by the stupidity of the question. And then, with an emphatic gesture, the fingers of his right hand splayed wide before his face, he signalled what was foremost in his mind.

. . . And now days, a great many of them, were burnt up,—the sun many times did sink beneath the western and well-defined elevations of earth. . . .

Evening. . . . The king drifted through the Hypostyle Hall on his sighs, walked along the shore of the Sacred

Lake in which orange flames, those of his torch-bearers, were reflected. The sounds of the sacred geese of the Great Cackler, as they settled into their nests, came from the aviary. . . . Now disconsolately the king went, wishing that the pathway he stepped over was that which led to the eyes, rather than simply to his vessel, which reaching he boarded and crossed over the river, soon found himself debarking at the very foot of his palace. He climbed steps, passed through passageways, and, in one of his audience chambers, on his way to the robe room, was waylaid by Nkuku, the steward, who spoke.

"Usermaatresetepenre, Born of Re, Father of Amun, God Ruler of Iunu, a guest is here for you to view."

"Eh?"

There were the whispers of agitated servants, the patter of feet.

"Just arrived this very evening from Mesopotamia," said the steward, "I present . . . Pigat . . . endowed with noble blood . . . the daughter of the daughter of Ammurapi, that last King of Ugarit."

And, from an adjacent chamber, a figure stepped forward. . . . Usermaatresetepenre opened his eyes wide. He thought that he was being confronted by some new form of goddess. Her nose was enormous, bulbous, deliciously mammiliform, so large indeed that it hid the rest of her face. . . . The two external openings to the nasal cavity (caverns into which he would willingly have leapt) were moist like those of a cow—their glistening nectar appeared more delicious than an ocean of honey-laced milk. . . . The object . . . so puffy . . . papillary . . . (a monument surpassing the highest pyramids in magnificence)

. . . was bewitching . . . of supreme and gynaecic beauty. . . . She was a veritable snout of heavenly worlds in female form.

"Ah," the king said, his whole body tingling with sensual anticipation, "at last I have found . . . this Great and Royal Consort;—and I will rub, my nose to hers,—even in the after-life!"

TOKYO

I.

THE CITY was a great hive, a mass of cells stacked one atop the next, these millions of habitations concealing each its own private comedy or pantomime—each its own stage. . . . With his thin, lithe fingers he stroked the plant's stem. He gently kissed the blossoms, the petals; sniffed at that sweet aroma . . . filaments, pistils now quivering. . . . As a boy Izō had seen a woman, beautiful, with a corsage at her breast, and had become strongly excited. . . . He was an intellectual, a voracious reader, and from Karr's *Les Fleurs Animées*, with the illustrations of Jean Ignace Isidore Gérard, he had moved to other things, ancient Greek tales: the tears of Asterea, the nymph called Anemone.

He found no pleasure in visiting white-fleshed masseuses or the bars of Ni-Chōme. In April he would wander through the Ueno Imperial Park and watch the cherry blossoms and the peonies. Being well off, with no need of employment, his time was his own;—to visit the

National Museum, view Bompō's painting of orchids; the red and white hibiscuses of Li Di; and then their wonderful collection of Jingdezhen ware, with magnolia and lotus designs.

His father disapproved of his life fervently.

"You need real employment," said his brother, a businessman of some importance.

Izō ran his fingers through the long black hair which descended from his scalp. "I grow flowers," was his response.

And the little greenhouse he had set up on top of his apartment building was indeed a collection of the most exquisite blooms. The Leopard Flower . . . Campanula, whose blossoms appeared like human lips . . . the charming yellow petals of Dancing Girl Ginger . . . Spanish Snapdragon . . . the fragrant Monkeytail Plant . . .

II.

His floors were covered with chintz printed with designs of poppies on a white background. He had a precious bamboo flower vase made by the hands of Sen no Rikyū.

At night, while sipping American whisky, he leafed through an old translation of Herr Sprengel's *The Newly Revealed Mystery of Nature in the Structure and Fertilization of Flowers*, his thoughts drifting over the bridal bed of soft, colourful petals, exquisitely perfumed, testicuii opening up, pouring out pulverum genitalem, cascades of which descend upon the tubam.

The clock struck ten.
He recited Bashō's poem:

Temple bells expire.
The fragrant blossoms remain.
An ideal evening!

III.

Yet he felt not entirely fulfilled. Looking for compan-
ionship, he would sometimes go to the Yumenoshima
Greenhouse Dome, next to, facilitated by, the Shin-Kōtō
Incineration Plant. There his vision rested on Lobster
Claw Heliconia . . . on Red Powder Puff . . . on a very
pretty orchid. . . . To drink from the bowl of her blossom. . . . Ah, if he could have a bride such as that, her
skin soft as eternal spring, what beautiful children they
would make!
    . . . colours and unending forms . . . . . .
The scent of a maiden.

IV.

Ginza. Blazing. Electrographics. The numerous neon
lights, in comancheite red, Naples yellow and manganese
blue, were themselves like so many bright flowers, opening their petals, flashing their stamens; and he walked
along the crowded street. His eyes wandered over the
window displays; he stopped, looked at an exhibit of
avant-garde fashions.

"Hello Izō!"

He turned his head, surprised to hear his name called out in that jungle. It was Mika, his brother's secretary. In the crook of her arm sat a large bunch of roses.

"Hello," he said. "Where are you going with those?"

She laughed. "Oh, I am just going home. I bought them for myself—for my apartment, to cheer it up. . . . And you, what are you doing?"

"Maybe I will get a bite to eat." He gazed at the flowers. "Would you like to join me?"

She smiled. Izō was normally so shy.

"Or you could come with me," she said. "I have food at my place."

———

"Where are they?"

"They?"

" . . . flowers."

"You saw. I put them in the vase."

"Bring them here, near us."

V.

Nothing seemed satisfactory; it never met his true and efflorescent ideal.

"Oh," he thought, "if only I could *really* be with her of the red cap, her of the long stem whose body smells like cinnamon;—to touch and to hold . . . an acacia flower with its autolytic aroma like that of an only just disgorged bottle of Perrier-Joüet Grand Brut;—even a floret to call my own, and make endless . . . endlessly . . . pollinate . . ."

He went to his greenhouse, looked over them: lust-petaled, desire-hued. He cut an exquisite bouquet and, soon after, climbed into bed with it, murmuring to himself those lines of Kikaku:

> Over the long road
> the flower-bearer pursues:
> abundant moonlight.

UBERLÂNDIA

"YOUR husband is a pig."

"And your point is?"

"You are such an attractive woman. I don't see the reason for such eccentricity."

It was true that Cintia, if not beautiful, was certainly attractive. Though her face tended towards the plain, her body was a gift from God—something that seemed stolen from the sun and rolling hills—grabbed from waterfalls and moonbeams.

The two women sat at the Bar Lou Lou on the Rua Goias. They sipped at glasses of cold beer and watched the palm trees sweat in the heat.

Fernanda was five or six years older than her friend. Her lips, smeared with paint, made her mouth look like some gorgeous fruit. That this organ was flanked by two puffy, over-powdered cheeks only accentuated its novelty.

"Don't get me wrong," she continued, the words slipping from between her lips like blood from a wound, "I love males of all sorts. But you, my dear, have taken things too far."

"João is a good one," Cintia said quietly. "And, any-how, can a woman ever resist her own heart?"

"Are you sure that it is your heart that's speaking?"

"Quite positive."

When she got home that evening João was in a sour mood. His only response to the kiss she placed on his brow was a sullen grunt. She fixed him a dinner of feijão e arroz. He shoved his snout in his bowl and ate with vigour, his eyes brightening somewhat.

Cintia's sister had once told her, "You must teach your husband to eat. He doesn't even know how to use a knife and fork!"

But she had just shrugged her shoulders without replying. If that sort of thing was important to other women, so be it. For her, she liked a man who was an animal.

He was extraordinarily fat and remarkably strong, his hair short and bristly, his eyes small and near-sighted.

It was true, other women's husbands would take them to the movies, dancing—on trips to the capitol or the seaside. But what of it? She had no need for waves or long bus rides. Uberlândia, with its jagged outline of buildings against a blue sky, was her home and lacked nothing. And what he himself lacked in social skills, he certainly made up for in other ways.

The next few days were happy ones—happy as they had been throughout the whole of that their first year together.

But then, as the week fell away, as January turned to February, she began to notice subtle changes in his behaviour. He seemed somewhat distant—his mind on other things. Her feathery laughter no longer ignited the subdued lightning-flash of his eyes.

She worked on the Avenida Afonso Pena, at the Riachuelo department store—selling pyjamas, blouses, socks, stockings and sunglasses.

One day, business being slow, she was allowed to go home from work a few hours earlier than usual.

She opened the door and was surprised to find Fernanda on her knees, her bright red lips pressed against João's snout.

"What is going on here?!?" Cintia cried.

Her friend got up and tucked her head down with false timidity.

"Well, my dear, can you really blame me?" she said. "After all your advertising, I had to see just what it was you found in him."

"Ah!"

"And, I must say," she faltered, with a vague smile playing around her lips, "that your sentiments for this fellow are fully justified."

The women stood silent, embarrassed, their gazes resting on João—that fat and strong fellow, with short, bristly hair.

He grunted; rubbed against one woman's leg and then the next, glanced at them both in a significant way.

"Oh, you pig!" they both cried out simultaneously.

VANCOUVER

GEORGI kept his hands in his pockets and with them could feel the movement of the muscles of his thighs. The cigarette lighter was there too and, with one hand, he clenched it and thought of a ploughed field, furrows, and the herbage that might sprout therein, after ample rain;—the point. His other five fingers ran along, and one of them felt that.

The park was beautiful and the sky clear overhead. Yet there were such things as ghosts and desolate wastes. The green hillock might just as well have been a sand dune in which to stick his head, and suffocate; the arbours, abrasive crags; the swan-studded pool, a festering swamp, from which rotting flesh is dredged. . . . Certainly, at least, Georgi's steps, in their morbid drag, reflected only the latter sentiments.

His face was handsome, though troubled with two days growth of whiskers, and his clothing elegant. He was young and obviously of nervous temperament.

He clasped the lighter tightly and flicked it in his pocket. —He remembered her, that head of long black hair; dark as iron oxide, or the soil of mars. Yes, her body might very well have been repulsive; and that face, as a skull might look bound in soiled linen. But what did it matter? Fibres, tendrils, gossamer. . . . The veins ran along his white wrists and quickened the flow of that thin, blue liquid.

People walked in the park, and some, probably young and innocent enough boys, shouted in its farthest regions. There was grass in which to sit and bushes in which to hide and benches on which to read. In the tennis court two men played. They both wore white. The ball clicked, rhythmically, between the two rackets. Interruption;—one man missed and both stopped, shouted and joked.

Georgi ground his teeth and tensed his jaw. Every pore of his scalp felt as if under attack,—by the stingers of ten thousand ominous insects.

But salvation stepped before him, in that ligulate wing, that dangling, swaying mane.

Let him move lightly.

She walked unaware, along the path that led through the grass. There was the other, who had worn it down as far as her derrière; so tractile, and worthy of his quivering lips. It was a terrible fever, and for days he had lain in mortal danger, a wet rag smoking on his forehead. How happy his family had been to see him sit up, and swallow a few spoonfuls of soup.

And during the long recovery, he had sat, stroking the cat, eyes glazed and wormed with threads of carnation. The Lamp Lighter Inn. . . . A rabbit's foot. . . . Fingers coursing through nocturnal locks.

He lunged, clasping the shears in his manic talons, and, with great rapidity, clipped off that flow of dark silk. . . . The shriek sounded as he ran over the green mounds and vaulted the shrubs. There would always be her, and that head of long, black hair, which had been her single beauty, and livelihood.

WARSAW

JACEK, the driver of the cab, was silent. He was willing to make conversation if provoked, but by no means inclined to instigate it. He took notice of the passenger through the rear-view mirror and developed certain opinions about the man. That there was a tragedy in the back seat he knew. The bald cranium, the flashing, deep-set eyes and loose flesh hanging from the jowl; these things spoke.

Jan hardly knew what ground he covered. He moved through the night, through the long, regular streets of the city, and this was all that mattered. Every new instant superseded that which had come before and sharpened the quintessence of his life. That final point was what he aimed for. All would be done and beautiful. Fulfilment, it had always been the answer.

Toothed. Some great veteran of love.

He crossed one leg over the next and smiled weakly. Who could understand such a true spirit as he? Only the very young, he thought.

"211 you said, right?" Jacek asked, turning halfway round in his seat.

"Yes. . . . We're here are we? . . . Good. I will call you later. In a few hours I imagine. To pick me up."

Jan handed the driver an amount significantly over that specified and climbed out onto the street.

Yes, 211, there was the address. Dr. Fogg would be expecting him. Behind those small, oval windows were answers, and of course gratification, in the extreme sense.

In a half daze he walked over a patch of dirt and weeds that served as a lawn, ignoring the walkway. He paid special attention to the sound of his feet beneath him. At the doorway he licked his lips and knocked. It opened and he was let in and saw the face that was to help him, deliver him to the tip of clandestine pleasure.

"Dr. Fogg . . ."

"Yes, Jan, I have been waiting for you."

The doctor's lips could not be translated behind the sporadic growth of moustache and beard. Jan hoped, and let himself believe, that they wore a comforting expression, something related to a smile.

"This way, and you can undress."

He followed the short figure into a back bedroom and took note of the unpleasant chemical odour. Whether it came from the doctor or the environment he could not tell, but he had smelled many striking odours in his life and was not easily discomfited.

Once naked, he lay on the bed, exposed and absolutely vulnerable.

"Will you hurt me?" he asked.

"Not unless you want me too," replied Dr. Fogg. "I was planning on using anaesthesia. It might cost you a little more, but I think it would be better."

"Yes. Please."

He drank in the gas offered him as if it were wine. He knew what he wanted, and the honing was sacred to him. He agitated and saw the doctor's eyes look down upon him.

"My practitioner . . . laughed . . . when I told . . . requested," Jan mumbled with a numb tongue.

Half conscious, he felt the vibration and heard the sawing. The flesh of his thigh seemed to be whipped and pulled away in strands. An aculeated man, a caterpillar; out of this chrysalis would he not emerge a butterfly, a piece of masculine cutlery?

"You have been unconscious for a long time," the doctor said.

"Was it a success?"

"You can see for yourself."

"Yes," Jan gasped, looking down. "It's gone."

"It's in the bathtub. Would you like to take it with you?"

"No. I want to be a spike."

The throbbing came when he got dressed, and became more pronounced as he paid and waited for the cab. Jacek helped him into the back seat without comment. The driver had seen many strange things at night, and did not need or care to know the answers.

Jan once again moved through the darkness. He knew that the nocturnal side of his life was not a total secret.

"They dismissed me without due consideration," he thought. "The board did not understand, did not remember Socrates or comprehend the teacher's prerogative."

The car passed under a street lamp and the back seat was flooded with short-lived light. He noticed the remaining limb, a dark and mystical slash, and a surge of dull pain swept up from the raw place. His teeth tingled from the very agony, which was so intense that he believed he could smell and taste it. Then they floated over a bridge, over the Vistula.

Later he found himself lying on his own bed, at home. He looked across at the bookshelf, full of the poetry he had once fed on. This was the place where he conducted his life, and it offered a vapid, almost hallucinatory comfort.

In India they worshipped things like him and offered oblations of ghee. There, in Poland, he had been jailed for this religion of his, this pagan obsession, and the playground shattered.

The hairless surface of his head was beaded with sweat. The rubbery effect of the drug Dr. Fogg had applied had vanished some time ago, he knew not when. That there was light outside and the vague outline of trees, was not so much a fact as a distorted semblance of reality; for the trill of birds took on accents of mocking little devils and the broken light that fell across the room flickered like flames.

He felt the bandage moist with pus and more and his whole body a long fibre of waning and warped virility.

"Single, single, single," he thought. "Straight and single."

It wracked him in a sensual hybrid of pain. He thought of rakes and hoes and shovels, cucumbers and carrots.

"Oh God," he thought as he expired. "I am a tusk."

XI'AN

IT was around 5:00 p.m. on a hot summer day. The police, having received a report of indecency, burst into the apartment of Yao Fa, a thirty-nine year old postal worker, who lived on Jinhualu. They found him wearing a curly mid-length blonde synthetic wig. Aside from that, he was completely naked. Upon searching the apartment, they discovered numerous other wigs, of every make and description. Over three hundred of them were counted. Mr. Yao was arrested. Later, upon being questioned, he said that he found great pleasure in putting on wigs and looking at himself in the mirror. No further explanation of his behaviour was given.

YEREVAN

IN mid-summer, when her catkins would appear, Mr. Vorperian was filled with a sense of wonder and would inhale the heavy odour with joy.

Leaves, shoots and branches, were all to him beautiful and felt he amorous impulses every time the tree he touched, behind the high walls of his yard.

He had a thick beard and would rub it against the trunk.

He ate, drank, snored, all the while thinking of it.

In summer, he enjoyed its shade; in fall, its nuts; in winter, its stark beauty; in spring, its new shoots.

"Why do I love you so much?"

It would have been better if he had left these words unsaid.

When a storm came, lightning struck strongly and the tree gave up its life.

Now he sits sad as a dusty chair before the fire.

The leaves had given him shade, the nuts had provided food, the wood now produced warmth.

ZÜRICH

MIDDLE AGED, a beautiful yellow silk tie apparent beneath his white lab coat, penetrating eyes, a refined nose resting atop a well-kept moustache; Ernest Wyss was the lead flavourist at Zwingli Corp—foremost innovator, creator and supplier of NI (natural identical) flavours in the world. Though the main production facilities were located on the edge of town, Wyss had his offices and laboratory in the centre, on Beethovenstrasse.

A maze of glass tubing and hoses. A forest of mixers, pumps and metres. He fiddled with trans-2-hexenal, eugenol and pentyl-iso valerate. He moved from the extraction equipment to the separation systems to his complex series of analysis instruments. Though he had two excellent industrial robots, he could not trust them with the delicate task he was involved in that day. For success in this enterprise would not only be certain to add billions of francs in market capitalization to the Corporation, but would also be the platinum crown of his own achievements.

He had always been a trend setter. It was he who had invented 2-methoxy-4-vinylphenol, that spicy-clovy-smoky flavour so essential for artificial bacon; and his 2-methyl tetrahydrothiophen-3-one (2-methyl-4, 5-dihydro(2H)3-thiophenone)—or blackcurrant—had revolutionised the artificial flavour industry. The most delicate sensations he had been able to synthetically ascertain—fuzzy peach skin, filberts, 2-isobutyl 4,5-dimethyl thiazole with its rose and geranium notes. He had conjured up wonderful strawberry flavours and delightful flavours of pineapple; had himself invented over two hundred varieties of cherry taste. His mountain mint was widely hailed as a masterpiece. Like God, he was a creator.

He had spent months patiently working on his latest product—adding a millionth part 4,4a,5,6,7,8-hexahydro-6-isopropenyl-4,4a-dimethyl-2(3H)naphthalenone, exchanging a hundredth part phenylethyl isothiocyanate for a three-hundredth methyl 3-nonenoate. But still he was frustrated in his endeavour. The product was never quite what it should have been—and indeed was turning into a real challenge.

"So near, yet so distant," he sighed.

The burden of genius was heavy.

It was time for lunch.

He removed his lab coat, put on a sports jacket and left the building.

He walked with short, careful steps down General Guisan-Quai, abstracted. To his right the lake shimmered beneath the mane of the May sun. He turned left, towards the Fraumünster. The streets were full of people.

Well dressed. Distinguished looking man in blueberry-coloured sweater gripping hand of young woman—maybe wife. An elderly gentleman follows his cane. A thick-necked blonde balances on the points of her heels—ever attentive lest they get caught in the cracks of the cobblestones.

Perfumed wealth (reeking obscenity) vied with costume-coated ugliness.

Zunfthaus zur Waag.

A robust and unsymmetrical waitress showed him to a table.

He looked over the menu.

"Schnitzel . . . spätzle . . . herring in double cream . . . rösti . . . calf's liver. Calf's liver. I have not had that in some time."

He ordered a plate of calf's liver, potatoes, kraut and a glass of beer. The waitress exhibited her teeth. He took a drink of his beer, letting the edge of his carefully tended moustache take on a fringe of white foam. Then his food. He allowed the aroma to arise into the wide cavities of his nostrils.

"Natural potatoes," he murmured, not in the least approving of the stuff's organoleptic characteristics. "They would have done better to add a little 3-(methylthio)butanal. After all, a potato without a methional homolog doesn't taste quite like a potato."

He chewed on the liver, his taste buds admiring greatly the heavy onion-garlic note with which the meat was adorned. Multi-layered vegetable strong-scented liliaceous plant stirring inner fire. Several efferent neural pathways were activated of a profoundly tender nature.

He found his eyes straying around the room, of their own accord—admiring—the heavy wooden furniture—the waitress's thick hips—silverware;—(he snorted out hot air). Esculent theopneusty. Revelatory aphrodisia. His microvilli were enchanted.

"The saddle is on the right horse!"

Ernest Wyss raised his eyebrows, threw down his napkin and paid the bill.

Everything in life is chemistry.

Back at the lab:

Beakers, phials, danced in his hands. He worked in the heat of inspiration. . . . Retracing territory he had already gone over a dozen dozen times . . . but with the addition . . . of . . . 25 ppm dipropyl trisulfide, formula $C6H14S3$, molecular weight 182.36, that very powerful chemical with a diffusive onion-garlic frequency . . . then the ever versatile furfuryl methyl disulfide . . . used in port, liver, chicken, salami, chocolate, coffee, toffee, bread . . . molecular weight 160.25 . . . 0.02% . . .

Finally, towards evening, a beaker of pale yellow liquid sat before him. It emitted a faintly sweet odour of melons, goats and human sweat with hesperidian top tints.

Should he dilute it?

No.

He was too impatient to test his results.

Eyedropper.

A single drop rolled over the red flesh of his outstretched tongue.

Burning sensation of horseradish. His eyes revolved back in his head. He pushed forward his chest and drew back his shoulders. Apple skins. Peely. His jaw slackened in response to sweet juicy notes. Burnt corn high impact aldehydic caramelised monsoon of pungency volcanic eruption of buttered liver. The hairs on the back of his hands stood on end.

"Ah," he breathed. "Finally I have discovered the true flavour of love!"

He drooled.